15.95

Bravo,
Mia!

by
Laurence Yep

★ American Girl®

To Felicia Salinas, whose spirit I admire

Published by American Girl Publishing, Inc.
Copyright © 2008 by American Girl, LLC
Printed in China
08 09 10 11 12 LEO 10 9 8 7 6 5 4
Illustrations by Robert Papp

Questions or comments? Call 1-800-845-0005, visit our Web site at **americangirl.com,** or write to Customer Service, American Girl, 8400 Fairway Place, Middleton, WI 53562-0497.

The characters and events portrayed in this book are fictitious. Any similarity to real persons, living or dead, is coincidental and not intended by the author or illustrator.

Picture credits: page 124—© Mark E. Gibson/Corbis; p. 125—© Andrew Fox/Corbis; p. 126—© Bob Carey/Getty Images; p. 127—© Charles Gupton/Corbis; p. 128—© Tim Pannell/Corbis; p. 129—© T. Kruesselmann/zefa/Corbis.

With gratitude to Patti Kelley Criswell, MSW, and coach Tricia Offerdahl.

Cataloguing-in-Publication Data available from the Library of Congress.

Contents

Chapter 1: There's No Biz Like Squirrel Biz 1

Chapter 2: Squirrel Power 13

Chapter 3: These Boots Are Made for Skating 19

Chapter 4: The Real Competition 29

Chapter 5: The Coin of Destiny 42

Chapter 6: Family Hearts 49

Chapter 7: Fairy Godmothers 56

Chapter 8: The Oakville Arms 67

Chapter 9: Snug as Two Bugs in a Rug 73

Chapter 10: Practice 82

Chapter 11: The Skaters 95

Chapter 12: The Buzz 103

Chapter 13: The Routine 110

Chapter 14: The Start 117

Real Girls, Real Letters 123

1

There's No Biz Like Squirrel Biz

Here's how to go from girl to squirrel in one easy lesson: Be in the wrong place at the wrong time—and be the wrong height. One moment my only worry was arriving on time at the rink, and the next thing I knew I had a four-foot gray tail sprouting from my back and an overbite that Dracula would envy.

That Saturday, when my brothers and I headed for the Lucerne Ice Arena, the last thing on my mind was changing species. I was looking forward to taking a break from preparing for Regionals. Competing there was my reward for doing well at my skate club's winter show last January, and Coach Schubert—yes, *the* Emma Schubert, the Olympic skater herself—had been training me pretty hard for the last eight months.

For just one day, I was supposed to concentrate on cleanup rather than on double jumps. A chain of stores called Nelda's Notions was celebrating its fortieth anniversary by offering free skating and free food for everyone at the Lucerne Ice Arena. There were also prizes for the best costumes—sewn, of course, from the stores' patterns.

The highlight of the party was to be a personal appearance by none other than Zuzu the Squirrel, and I was really looking forward to meeting her. Zuzu is the mascot for Nelda's Notions stores, and she is *everywhere*. When my parents were kids, they watched Zuzu's cartoon show on television every day after school. The show's no longer on, but Zuzu still performs at schools and events like this, and she is a daily presence in advertisements in newspapers and on television and radio.

However, as my brothers and I walked unsuspectingly through the front door, surrounded by witches, pirates, and zombies, Coach Schubert pounced on us. Well, on *me*, anyway.

"What do you think, Nelda? Will she do?" the coach asked over her shoulder.

Nelda is the owner of Nelda's Notions, and she's different from every adult I know. She's in her sixties, and her white hair is permed and cut into an upside-down bowl shape, which always makes me think of a tall mushroom. As always, she was dressed all in pink, from the scarf around her neck to her fuzzy sweater to her slacks and boots.

"You've got a good eye for size, Emma." Nelda nodded. "You're right—she's Zuzu to a T." And then she eyed my brothers. "And a bonus. You three look like certified elf material if I ever saw it."

The coach patted me on the back as she sent me off with Nelda. "Don't worry about cleanup today. I'll find someone else to handle it."

The next thing I knew, Nelda was ushering us to the rink's backstage area, where I climbed into a squirrel outfit and my brothers were given elf ears.

Nelda said that the person who regularly plays Zuzu had sprained an ankle on the way to the rink. When Coach Schubert heard about the problem and saw the costume, she estimated that I was the right size, and volunteered me.

So suddenly there I was, trying to stand up—on skates!—in a giant squirrel costume. My body felt all wrong. I was at least a foot taller and a couple of feet wider, and I had so much extra weight around my waist that I swayed and shifted unexpectedly. And don't even ask me what my tail was doing.

It was dark inside the costume, too, so I felt as if I had been swallowed by a giant squirrel. My only opening onto the world was the little mesh window beneath the muzzle. I kept looking down through the window, but I couldn't see my feet, only the white fur of my bulging squirrel tummy. How was I going to walk, let alone skate?

The only things that kept me from . . . well . . . going *squirrelly* were my brothers, Perry and Skip, who were holding on to me on either side. That was a lot of support since Perry, who's seventeen, is as tall as a sky-scraper and Skip, at fifteen, is just a few stories shorter—that is, if skyscrapers had the pointed ears of elves.

Through the mesh window, I saw my youngest brother, Rick, standing by the curtains that separate the backstage area from the rink. At thirteen, he's two years older than I am. Like my other brothers, he was wearing elf ears that stuck up like spikes. I would have teased him, but it's hard for someone in a squirrel suit to make fun of someone merely in elf ears. When it came to who looked silliest, I won paws down.

Suddenly Nelda's smiling face appeared in front of the mesh window. "Now, don't be nervous, hon," she reassured me. "Zuzu will handle all the cuteness for you. All you have to do is stay upright." She gave me a big hug. "And thanks for doing this. Zuzu's fans would have been so upset if she had missed this party, and so would Zuzu."

The voice of Bob Gunderson, who is the rink

superintendent and my good friend, boomed over the Lucerne's speakers, "And now, the moment you've all been waiting for: it's time for everyone's favorite, fantastic, fantabulous furry friend . . ."

At his cue, Rick drew one side of the curtains apart.

Nelda gave me a little push. "Go on, hon. Make Zuzu proud!"

"Ladies, gentlemen, and children of all ages, Zuzu is *in* the building!" Bob thundered, and then he played Zuzu's jingle:

"We're just nuts about sewing."

Slowly, carefully, I skated forward to meet my— I mean *Zuzu's*—public. After only a couple of steps, I began to think that just remaining upright might be too much of a challenge for me.

The weight of Zuzu's large tail pulled me backward, so I had to lean forward slightly to compensate. And when the costume's head and the body started to sway in one direction, they wanted to keep going that way. I had to adjust constantly to keep my balance.

I wasn't worried about getting hurt if I fell. Nelda had assured me that there was so much padding in the costume that it was like having a mattress wrapped around me. But we squirrels have our pride. I didn't want anyone to think that Zuzu was clumsy.

As soon as my brothers saw me struggling, they slid up on either side and took hold of my paws, leading me out into the rink. Immediately, applause began echoing against the walls and ceiling. People had clapped for me at the Lucerne's winter show last January, but not like this. This was like a warm, invisible wave from the whole town that rolled toward me—well, not the me who was Mia, but the me who was Zuzu.

"Incoming skaters," Skip warned.

I couldn't see Zuzu's fans at first, but I could hear them dimly through Zuzu's huge head. Dozens and dozens of skates were hissing across the ice toward me. I sometimes help out with the beginners' skating class, the Twinkles, so I recognized the short, staccato rhythm little kids make when they try to skate.

"Take your positions," Perry ordered.

We weren't prepared for all the pirates, princesses, witches, vampires, and puppies that swarmed around us, but fortunately my brothers' hockey instincts took over. My brothers guarded my back and sides and intercepted Zuzu's fans as determinedly as if the kids were opponents with pucks trying to shoot a goal. They steered the kids so that they were in front of me where I could see them.

When one little girl, dressed as a fairy, saw me, she skidded to a halt, covered her mouth with her hands, and broke into happy giggles. Her parents smiled as if they were as pleased to meet me as their daughter was. As they escorted her away, I heard them telling their daughter how they had watched Zuzu on television when they were her age. They spoke about Zuzu as if she had been their friend since childhood.

When there was a momentary lull, Dad skated over. Mom was busy at home preparing for a bake sale for Rick's hockey team the next day, but Dad had volunteered to help at the rink. He was wearing an apron, so he must have been helping at the buffet.

"Mia, is that you?" he asked.

"*Ix-nay*, Dad," Perry whispered firmly, and then in a much louder voice he politely asked, "Would you like to meet Zuzu, sir?"

"I'd love to." Dad broke into a wide grin, just as the giggler's parents had.

When I raised my paw and shook his hand, he looked as pleased as any little kid—and as if he had forgotten for a moment that I was his daughter.

After Dad left, I must have posed for dozens of

pictures. The flashing of all those cameras made me feel like a star, and even though no one could see my face, I found myself smiling from ear to ear inside Zuzu's head. Was this what it felt like to be famous?

Okay, it was *Zuzu* who was the actual star—but I like to think that Zuzu is bighearted enough to share *some* of her glory with me.

After all, there's no biz like squirrel biz.

It was just a few minutes later that Vanessa Knowles skated past. Like me, she's eleven, but she is a far better skater. Her parents make sure she has whatever she wants, including the latest fashions and fanciest costumes. She seems to think that her parents' money entitles her to say whatever she likes, so almost everyone avoids her. She stopped, her lips curling up in a smirk. "Mia, is that you?"

Since I had a little boy standing by me, I figured it was okay to fib, and I shook my head emphatically.

"Can't you tell it's *Zuzu?*" Perry asked, trying to get her to play along.

Vanessa jabbed a finger at him and then at me. "If you're here, then that must be your sister." She looked straight at me. "The look's an improvement for you."

Through the mesh, I glanced at the little boy. To my relief, he was too busy playing with my paw to pay attention to Vanessa.

Before she could do any real harm, she was bumped to the side by a flood of costumed kids, all crying "Zuzu!" With an annoyed expression, Vanessa turned and skated away.

Unfortunately, there were now so many children on the ice that they overwhelmed my elves. Suddenly Zuzu was in danger of being loved to death as children tugged from all sides. When I moved to my left to maintain my balance, the suit was still jiggling to the right. I felt like a bowl of JELL-O in the middle of an avalanche and, just as I thought I was finally going to fall over, my friend Anya Sorokowski cried, "Oh, Zuzu! I've been dying to meet you!"

Anya's my best friend and the same age as I am. She stretched over all the little bobbing heads to wrap her arms around me—actually steadying me, although she was disguising it as a hug. Her face peered through the mesh window. "I thought it was you," she murmured, "because only you would get yourself stuck in a mess like this."

With Anya's help, my brothers managed to free

me from the mob of adoring fans.

Anya had brought her six-year-old sister, Alexandra, to see Zuzu. Alexandra was in a fancy pink princess costume, and at first I think she suspected I was her sister's friend, but then, with my elves keeping the other kids temporarily at a distance, something strange happened. I stopped feeling like I was wearing Zuzu's costume and felt more like Zuzu herself. I began playing patty-cake with Alexandra. She warmed instantly. Giggling like the other little girl had, she rocked on her skates with happy excitement. It was just as Nelda had said: Zuzu would handle the cuteness.

Suddenly I heard Nelda exclaim, "Oh, look at Zuzu with that little darling. Don't you want some footage of that?"

The next moment bright lights flooded the rink, and through the mesh opening I caught a glimpse of a man with a huge television camera that had the logo of the local television station. With him was a reporter, Lillian Chin, with a big microphone.

Lillian Chin asked me a question, but all I could do was give a big Zuzu-style shrug and wave to the camera. All the attention made Alexandra shy, so she scurried behind Anya.

Lillian Chin was trying to coax Alexandra into

coming forward again when Mayor Chuck "Chuckles" Weyberg roared over.

"My darling Zuzu!" he boomed. The music playing in the background must have inspired him, because he grabbed one of my paws and said, "I've had a crush on you, Zuzu, since I was a kid. How about a dance?"

Even if I could have protested, the mayor didn't give me a chance. The unexpected motion was too much, and although I struggled to keep my balance, I finally toppled like a furry tree. There was a solid *thunk* as Zuzu's big fiberglass head hit Mayor Chuck on his head, and we both fell together. I ended up landing on his chest.

I'd been falling on the ice and getting back to my feet my whole life, but never in a squirrel costume. I started to get up, but I lost my balance and fell back onto the mayor. Where were my elves?!

"Stop," Coach Schubert ordered, "before you flatten the mayor."

By now, when the coach said to do something, I automatically did it. So I stayed still, crouched on top of the mayor, suddenly aware that in addition to the TV camera trained on us, digital cameras were flashing, and all around us people were laughing.

As the coach helped me to my hindpaws again,

Bravo, Mia!

I heard someone shout, "Zuzu for Mayor!" And others took up the chant.

With a grimace, the mayor drew his hand across his throat in a slashing gesture, trying to signal the television crew to turn off its light and camera. But the light just kept on shining and the news camera kept on recording.

2

Squirrel Power

Nelda and Coach Schubert led me off the rink before I could knock over anyone else. It was a relief to take off the suit and get back to being me. I apologized to Nelda, but she just grinned as she handed me a sports drink. "Didn't you see all the folks? They loved it." When she was sure I was all right, she excused herself to get back to her guests, including Mayor Chuck.

I emptied the bottle and was about to go out and do my chores at the rink, but the coach caught up with me and told my brothers and me to go home.

"You've done enough today," she said with a chuckle. "Besides, I'm afraid that if you went out now, people would pay more attention to you than to Nelda's party, and today really ought to be about *her*. Or," she arched an eyebrow, "is there some other politician you want to crush?"

Dad left with us, bringing home some bags of goodies from the buffet, which he distributed among us to carry. As we walked the three blocks home from the rink, Skip peeked into the bag he was holding and smacked his lips. "I can't wait to dig in to all this stuff."

Free food was how I'd lured my brothers into going to the Lucerne in the first place. Between the expenses for my figure skating and my brothers' private hockey teams, our family budget is tight. Besides their regular jobs, both of my parents work part-time as well. Unfortunately, though, local companies are cutting back, so things are even tighter than usual for us right now because Dad's part-time job has shrunk to just a few hours a week.

Less money coming in means that our parents have cut back on everything, including our food budget. We aren't starving—not by a long shot—but my brothers are human vacuum cleaners who can practically suck up even the plates from the dinner table.

"Dad, did you include any nuts for Mia?" Perry teased.

Wincing, I said loudly, "Enough with the squirrel jokes, please."

"Or what?" Rick asked. "You'll bite us?"

I was tempted to do just that when kindhearted Skip tried to change the subject. "Did you see the princess outfit that Alexandra was wearing? It was like something from a musical."

"Lucky little girl to have such a nice costume." Rick started to laugh as he said, "Hey, remember that

Halloween when Mom tried to save money by making all our costumes? And the seams were so twisted that everything fit weird?"

Perry laughed, too, as he patted Rick between the shoulder blades. "You looked like a werewolf with a hunchback."

"Well, a hunchback wasn't as bad as having three ears, like Mia did." Skip jerked a thumb at me.

"Yeah," I agreed and glanced accusingly at Dad. "I wore that kitten outfit only because you fibbed and told me that it meant it was a special breed of cat." I added, "I got teased for a month afterwards."

Dad scratched his nose as he pretended a sudden fascination with the sky. "Did I? I'm afraid I don't quite remember."

"Mom does all right with a needle and thread, but she never got the knack of sewing those stretchy materials," Perry said.

"Like you would know which end of a needle to use," I said, defending her. "Stretch material is tricky stuff. Not everyone can handle it." I knew that because I had had my own catastrophes with sewing stretchy fabric.

"After that Halloween, you always went as ghosts," Dad chuckled.

"That's because all Mom had to do was cut holes in old sheets," Rick said.

Perry tugged at his ear as if he wanted to make sure it didn't have a point anymore. "Elves have even simpler costumes," he said and then sighed. "But appearing as an elf is not quite the way I wanted to celebrate." Just yesterday, we'd found out that Perry's hockey team had been invited to an important tournament, where only the very best teams would play. There would be plenty of college and professional scouts there. It was Perry's big chance.

"Look at it this way," Skip teased. "You could be the first elf ever to play hockey."

I started to salivate the moment we came in through the back door of our home. The kitchen smelled of fresh baking, and Mom was taking a sheet of cookies out of the oven.

Dad held his paper bag up triumphantly. "Beloved spouse, the foragers have returned!" he announced loudly over the talk show playing on the little black-and-white television on the counter.

"And a hearty welcome to you, equally beloved

spouse, and offspring." Mom set the cookie sheet on the stovetop as she looked at me. "I guess I don't have to ask you how your afternoon went." She paused and then added meaningfully, "*Zuzu.*"

I wanted to empty the leftovers from the paper bag in my hands and put the bag over my head. "How did you know?" I asked in a small voice.

"The phone's been ringing off the hook," Mom explained, "after people figured out you *had* to be Zuzu. I never knew I had such a talented daughter."

Suddenly the talk show was cut off abruptly by a sign on the television that said "Breaking news."

"And now we bring you an urgent news bulletin from Lillian Chin on location at the Lucerne Ice Arena," a voice said excitedly.

The next moment we were staring at Lillian Chin in front of the Lucerne. "Today," she said in a breathless voice, "Mayor Chuck Weyberg was viciously assaulted. Police are asking you to be on the lookout for a giant gray rodent with a large, fluffy tail and a huge overbite. She is considered quite dangerous." She suddenly smiled and added, "But only if you are a politician. The rest of us needn't worry."

I looked in horror at the television screen while the station kept replaying my fall, making it look as if

I were hopping up and down on the mayor as on a trampoline. The caption at the bottom of the screen read in big, bold letters: "Zuzu Debates the Mayor."

Then the camera panned to the skaters chanting, "Zuzu for Mayor."

Oh, yes, I would definitely be wearing that paper sack over my head when I went to school.

3

These Boots Are Made for Skating

Monday morning, I was looking forward to putting Zuzu and the mayor behind me by getting on the ice to practice for Regionals. At first, when Coach Schubert told me I would be going, I'd been thrilled—for all of one evening—and then the reality had set in.

We'd added one extra coaching session each week, which my family was just managing to handle. For the last eight months since getting the news, my stomach had been constantly in knots, my whole body ached from practice and training, and sometimes I had to sit at a tilt because my behind was bruised from all the falls.

With only a month to go until Regionals, I was still making a lot of mistakes, so I was feeling anxious enough without having my boots give me problems, too. It was hard to put them on, so I figured they had shrunk somehow. Frustrated, I just crammed my feet into them, determined to make the leather stretch again.

I got them on, but it hurt a little to walk in them. I didn't forget about the ache in my feet until I heard the *swish-swish-swish* of Coach Schubert's nylon pants.

I turned and saw that she was in the center of the rink, gliding effortlessly along the ice, her hair pulled up into a ponytail.

When she saw me, she skated over, stopping in a small shower of flakes. "A skater should be able to learn from any experience." A corner of her mouth turned up. "Like, how did it feel to be a celebrity for a day?"

I felt my face turning red with embarrassment. "I didn't mean to mug the mayor," I blurted out. "It was fun up until the mayor got into the act and we both went down. But the kids were great. You should have heard them when they met me. At least once in their lives, I hope everyone gets to feel what it's like to be Zuzu."

"Good," she said, clapping her hands together in approval, "because if you feel special, sometimes you skate special. The right audience can make you rise above your normal level. But that's not what I meant to ask. I've done my share of choreography for ice shows. What was it like *inside* the Zuzu suit?"

"Hot, stuffy . . ." I paused as I hunted in my memory. "The worst thing, though, was that it was hard to see—almost like skating blindfolded."

She fed me the next question, clearly already knowing the answer. "If you could have taken the head off, would it have been easy to skate?"

I shook my head. "No, the rest of the suit threw off my balance. And it only got worse when kids tugged on me."

The coach nodded. "Ever see those runners who train with weights on their ankles? They do that because when they take the weights off for an actual race, they feel so much lighter and can run faster. Let's see if it's something similar for you. Don't worry about skating the choreography when you hear the music. Just have fun with it."

I took the guards off my blades and stepped onto the ice as the coach put my music into the portable stereo system we use for practices. It always sits on top of the boards near the doorway.

Under that high roof, *Swan Lake* sounded tinny. But it didn't matter. I'd been living the music for the last eight months, and I knew it by heart.

It even scared me a little because I could never forget that the coach had been skating to it at the Olympics when she'd fallen and lost the gold medal.

I'd associated *Swan Lake* so much with working on my routine that I'd forgotten how lovely it is on its own. The music seemed to tug me out onto the ice, as if by invisible strings. And as I glided along without the

weight and darkness of Zuzu's costume, I felt almost
like I was flying. So I bent forward, spreading my arms
like wings, as if I were a real bird. For a wild, heady
moment, I felt like I could do anything, so, lifting one
leg behind me, I balanced on just one thin steel blade.

I thought of hawks I'd seen swooping gracefully
first to the right and then to the left—not to hunt but just
for the sheer joy of it. I cut elegant arcs in the ice as I
surged forward, leaning to one side and then the other.
I had never felt more in control of my balance, now that
I didn't have the outer skin of a squirrel shifting in
unexpected ways.

All too soon, the music ended, and I straightened
again and stopped with a grin.

The coach asked, "How do you feel?"

"Like I could do anything," I said cheerfully.

"Good. Try to keep some of that confidence when
you skate your routine now," she said and motioned for
me to take my place. "Sometimes you look like someone doing long division rather than skating."

"I'm just worried about messing up," I said as
I got into position.

"You've got too vivid an imagination. Don't
worry. Don't even think. Just let the music and your
body do it all for you this time," she instructed.

I tried to shut out all the imaginary calamities and just listen again. *Don't worry. Don't think,* I told myself.

As soon as I heard the first sweet notes, my muscles knew what to do before my brain could tell them. I was starting to enjoy myself when I tried to go into a flying camel spin and wound up doing a nose-dive into the ice.

"Get back up," the coach urged. "Keep going."

My double lutz is my other major problem. It always gives me trouble, and although I'd done it successfully in the winter show, I still wasn't landing it consistently. It didn't help either that my feet suddenly began aching inside my boots. It made me pause just a fraction of a second, but that was enough to throw off the timing of my jump, so I didn't leap high enough and I was barely through my second rotation before I started to descend. I fell hard and swept forward like a human dust rag.

"Up!" the coach ordered. "Finish the routine."

I once again rolled over onto my knees and turned as I rose. I was sure I had a bruise on my hip now, but I tried not to let all my aches distract me. I completed the rest of my routine, feeling less like a graceful hawk and more like a wallowing hippo.

The coach came over to brush some of the ice flakes from me. "Let's talk about the flying camel first. Do you know what a sweet spot on a baseball bat is?"

I knew that from P.E. class. "If you can hit the ball with that part of the bat, you make the ball go farther and harder."

The coach raised one boot and pointed at the curved skate blade near the front. "There's a sweet spot on a blade, as well, that lets you jump and spin better. It's just about beneath the ball of your foot. We'll work on helping you find that spot more often."

"Would that help with the double lutz, too?"

I asked hopefully.

"Somewhat, but you've got to keep your head to the right at takeoff and pull your arms and legs tighter," the coach explained. "If you do that, you'll be able to complete your rotations."

I managed to find the sweet spots on my blades, and true to the coach's word, it was easier to spin. Even so, I kept making other mistakes on my flying camel spin. And I continued to flub the double lutz.

At the end of practice, the coach had me skate my entire routine again, and I tried to recapture the wonder of those first few minutes of the day. However, it was as hopeless now as a groundhog trying to catch a jet plane. Even when I managed to stay upright, I made so many mistakes that I felt like the newest rookie.

"Sorry," I panted.

"If you tried your best, you have nothing to be sorry for," the coach called as she waved me off the ice.

"It felt so good at the start," I said as I moved toward her, "but then I lost it when I fell, and I never got it back, no matter what I did."

"Not every skater gets to experience that nice part," she said, "so count yourself lucky. And try to remember what it was like. It'll give you something to strive for." She suddenly looked up at the stands. "Well, what do you think, Nelda?" she called out.

"Not bad," Nelda said. As always, she was a vision in pink as she came down the steps. "She reminds me of someone else when she was this age."

"You were always there to encourage me, Nelda," the coach said. "And don't think I didn't appreciate it."

I still felt bad about the other day. "I hope I didn't ruin your anniversary party," I said once again to Nelda as I stepped onto the rubber mat behind the boards.

"Will you quit that?" she said, handing my skate guards to me. "I didn't come here for an apology. Zuzu and I like to keep tabs on our girls. You're part of a very exclusive club now: Once a Zuzu, always a Zuzu. You were the highlight of our party. In fact, you were the highlight of the news all across the country."

I felt as if my blood had just been replaced by ice water. "What?"

Nelda spread her hands and wriggled her fingers with their bright pink fingernails. "The local station fed that bit to stations around the country. I couldn't have bought that much publicity. Zuzu and I have invitations to do all sorts of talk shows on TV and radio."

"The mayor's going to hate this." I was sure he was going to close Nelda's Notions out of revenge.

"I've known Chuck since he was knee-high and

coming in to the shop with his mother and getting his sticky fingerprints all over my fabrics." Nelda winked. "He knows a good thing when it happens. He's even asked to pose with Zuzu for some campaign pictures." When she saw my panicked expression, she held up a hand. "Don't worry, hon. The regular actor's going to play Zuzu, but she'll never match your version."

"The mayor should feel relieved about that," I said with a small grin.

Now that I had finished practice and we were just standing there, my feet were starting to hurt again. I had to leave for school, but as I took a couple of steps, the coach stopped me. Bending, she pressed so hard on the toes of my boots that I winced.

"They shrank a little," I said hastily. "They'll be okay when I stretch them out."

The coach shook her head. "I should have noticed it before. You've grown out of your boots, and your cramped feet are throwing you off a bit. That might explain some of your hesitation. Better get a new pair right away so you can break them in before Regionals."

I think in the back of my mind I had known that, and I had just been pretending that it was a problem that I could fix by myself. I just didn't see how my parents could afford a new pair of boots for me right now.

Bravo, Mia!

Zuzu's hind paws had been roomy enough.
Maybe I could borrow *them* for Regionals.

4

The Real Competition

After school, I went back to the Lucerne to restock the shelves of the Snack Shack. While I was there, I looked at the used skating boots. Bob's wife, Mona, is the shop manager, and she helped me search. Unfortunately, there was nothing my size—and nothing I could have afforded anyway.

Still, Mona took my measurements and promised to keep an eye out for a pair. "I don't care how old or worn they are," I said, figuring that I might be able to scrape up enough cash for beat-up boots.

Mona gave me an indignant look. "Do you want to look scruffy at Regionals?" And then she promised, "I'll see that we do better than that."

Then I headed for the boardroom, where all the skaters who were going to Regionals were gathering for a meeting. As I slipped dejectedly into the seat next to Anya, she whispered to me, "What's wrong, Mia? You've been moping around all day."

"Money's tight, and so are my boots," I whispered.

She knew my family's problems. "Maybe you could borrow a pair of mine."

I'd thought of that, but Anya's a lot smaller than I am. "Thanks, but if I could fit into yours, I could fit into mine."

"Well," Anya joked, "my mom has a recipe for pickling cucumbers. You ought to see how that stuff shrinks them."

I jiggled my shoes. "I'm sure my family would love it if I smelled like pickles. But hey, don't worry. I'll figure out something before Regionals."

My parents weren't sure if they could make it to Regionals for the whole time, so Anya and her mother had offered to take me with them and have me stay in their room. "I'm counting on having you there for moral support," Anya whispered.

Anya can skate as well as anyone in practice or in an exhibition like the last winter show, but she seems to fall apart in competition.

Before I could reassure Anya, Coach Schubert strode into the room and took a moment to survey the ten of us. We were the first group she was taking from the club to Regionals, and we ranged from senior-level skaters like Chad and Izumi to Anya and me—and Vanessa—on the bottom rung. The skaters on the levels above us would move on to Sectionals if they placed in the top three, but our event was nonqualifying, so there

"I'm counting on having you there for moral support," Anya whispered.

was no next step in the competition. We were going just to gain experience.

"Excited?" Coach Schubert asked.

The other skaters nodded their heads and murmured, but I just sat there, my stomach doing somersaults at the mere thought of Regionals.

"Well, you're not as excited as I am," the coach insisted. "First of all, I want to thank you." We glanced at one another, puzzled, as she went on. "I feel so lucky having skaters like you."

Grinning at one another, we began to relax in our seats and the coach smiled, too. "So let's enjoy every moment together. But I also want to warn those of you who are going for the first time: you're going to be on a much larger stage than you are here at the Lucerne, so you'll have a lot to adjust to." She glanced at Chad and Izumi. "Those skaters who have been there before, I hope you'll help the rookies."

Izumi merely nodded, but Chad turned to look around the room. "Sure, feel free to ask me anything."

"What's your cell phone number?" one of the older girls called out.

Chad blushed as the rest of us laughed. The coach waited a moment before she held up her hands again for quiet. "Everyone in this room has the physical skills needed to stand on the podium. Those are the skills that you've developed here and that have made you stand out."

She paused significantly before she resumed. "However, at Regionals you're going to go up against other skaters who are every bit as good as you are physically." It was silent in the room while we all chewed on that.

"So what's going to separate you from the pack?" She tapped at her temple. "It's here inside your head. It's how you handle the enormous pressures you're all going to face during that competition. You'll develop those mental skills faster competing at Regionals than you can here at the Lucerne. That's a *big* reason to go. Just remember your training, and keep your focus on your routine. Competition is as much about mental toughness as it is about physical strength and grace. The lessons you'll learn at Regionals will serve you well, whether you pursue skating as a career or go into other things."

She straightened. "But I repeat: I wouldn't take you if I didn't think you could win." She rapped a knuckle on a table to emphasize each word. "What's really important is that you learn from this experience so that you can be even better the next time. Because—"

she turned so she could look at each of us in turn—
"you're all excellent skaters, so there *will* be a next
time. And that's a promise."

As the room started to buzz, she went on. "One
more thing. Be aware that you're going to be judged off
the ice as much as on it. So please be sure to dress and
behave appropriately at all times."

"Better stay away from the sequins, Vanessa," a
boy called Tyler snickered from the back of the room.
At our winter show, Vanessa's costume had shed beads
and sequins all over the ice, causing her to trip and fall.

Vanessa whipped around in her chair to scowl at
him. "That wasn't my fault. It was . . ." Her voice faltered.

Everyone looked nervously at the coach, because
Vanessa and her parents blamed the coach for not
having checked Vanessa's dress first—even though
Vanessa's self-designed outfit had arrived only hours
before the show. Vanessa's influential parents had been
against hiring Coach Schubert in the first place, and
they were still trying to find an excuse to get her fired.

Vanessa said nothing more, but you didn't have
to be a mind reader to know what she was thinking as
she stared back at Coach Schubert.

The coach ignored her, though, so that she could
fasten her gaze on Tyler. "You will treat each other

with courtesy and respect at all times. Or you will stay behind. Do you understand me?" He sank in his chair, looking as if he wished he could hide somewhere. "Even though you're competing individually, sometimes against one another, you are still part of a team. Together you represent the Lucerne Skate Club. Never forget that."

I think we all felt that things were going to be just fine as long as we had Coach Schubert in our corner.

After the coach's pep talk, I resolved to do my strengthening and flexibility exercises, even though I usually find them boring. I rushed home to get started before everyone came home for dinner. However, when I walked through the front door of our house, I stopped when I heard all the noise. The furnace was rattling louder than usual. It was so bad that I stood there for a moment, trying to decide if it was just that or if there was also someone banging around in the back of the closet—because there shouldn't have been. We keep a chart with everyone's schedule, and I knew that I should be the only one home right now.

I grabbed the telephone on the table by the door,

in case I needed to dial 911. The thumps moved from the back of the closet toward me, and the coats by the doorway began to move. Frightened, I raised the receiver to use it as a club.

"Is it something I said?" Mom asked as she came out of the closet on a pair of crutches, one hand awkwardly clutching a feather duster. "Or do you greet everyone in your family this way?"

Sheepishly, I put the receiver back into the cradle. "What happened, Mom?"

She nodded down at the cast on her leg. "I took a bad tumble at work this morning. Sarah took me to the hospital and dropped me back here an hour ago." Sarah's one of Mom's coworkers. "Your dad's driving his boss into the city and couldn't get back in time."

I snatched the feather duster from her. "You just broke your leg? You should be lying down in bed—or at least on the sofa. Not cleaning! Does it—does your leg hurt a lot?"

"Not right now," Mom said. "And I *was* lying down, but I was having trouble resting with the house such a mess. There's so much to do around here that it's driving me a little crazy."

I decided that my exercises and homework could wait until later. I motioned Mom toward the sofa. "Let me handle this. You just sit."

I pulled a pile of newspapers and a basket of clean laundry off the couch so that she could rest. Then I grabbed a pencil and paper. "Let's make a list. What needs to be done, beginning with the most important?"

As the list grew longer, I realized how much Mom does, and how much we all take her for granted. "How do you do it all?" I asked when she was finally done. "How do you balance all this with your jobs— and our sports?"

Mom gave a little shrug. "I've learned to focus on what has to be done at a given moment. I just tell myself to take it one step at a time. But lying here doing nothing, it all got to be a bit overwhelming. Which is why I tried to start dusting. Pretty goofy of me, I guess." Mom shook her head and laughed at herself. "But tell me about *your* day, Mia."

I started to say something about needing new skate boots, but I stopped. Mom didn't need one more thing to worry about at this particular moment, and that could wait until later. Right now, I just wanted to see Mom smile, so before I tackled the list, I intended to give her a big dose of TLC.

First, I made her as comfy as I could, plumping up cushions beneath her head and under her cast. The house was colder than usual, so I put a blanket over her legs. Then I continued to pick up until the living and dining rooms were, if not spotless, at least neater.

"You know," I said, talking in a loud voice so that I could be heard over the banging of the furnace, "Grandmom always says that there's a silver lining to every cloud. Since you're going to have to stay home, we'll get to do more things together."

Mom perked up. "Sure, just us girls."

"I'll borrow some movies from the library for us," I said, growing excited at the prospect. She and I are often outvoted on film choices by the males in the family, although we sometimes force the boys to watch a musical with us.

Mom nodded in agreement. "It'd be nice to see a show that didn't involve cars crashing or buildings blowing up." She clasped my hand suddenly. "And because the doctor doesn't want me to go back to work right away, I was thinking that maybe I could go to Regionals with you. I'm sure Mrs. Sorokowski and Anya wouldn't mind sharing their room with me, too."

"You mean you'd be there with me the *whole* time?" I asked.

Mom grinned and nodded. "Instead of just driving up on the day of the competition with your dad and the boys."

"I'd really love that," I said cautiously, "but can you really do it?"

"You couldn't keep me away," she insisted.

I still didn't know what to do about my skates, but I wasn't about to let something like that keep me from taking a trip with Mom.

"We had a meeting today, and Coach Schubert said we should dress nicely off the ice as well as on it," I said. "So what do you think I should wear?" I usually like to make my own choices now, but I thought Mom would enjoy giving me her opinion.

I had expected Mom to talk it through while she lay on the sofa, but she immediately insisted on clumping up to my bedroom to check out my wardrobe personally. I managed to make her lie down on my bed while I took various things from my closet and drawers.

Mom's part-time job at a boutique lets her get some very nice things for me at a discount, so I knew I wouldn't be an embarrassment to the skating club. Mom wanted to see everything I had, so she kept me hopping as she had me try on different outfits, mixing and matching.

Mom sighed happily, "This is so fun, Mia, and we don't get to do this very often. Don't get me wrong. I love the boys, but I'm grateful that I finally had a girl, too."

I laughed. "Yeah, their idea of high fashion is a new sweatshirt."

Mom pointed at my green skating dress. "Try it on," she urged. "I always enjoy seeing you in it."

That wasn't any burden, because I wanted to put it on. I hadn't worn it since January. But now it was snug in all the wrong places. *First the boots, now the dress,* I complained to myself. *Why does my whole outfit have to pick on me?*

Worry lines appeared on Mom's forehead. "Stop tugging, dear. You'll tear it."

"I've almost got it on," I said, trying to wriggle into it.

"No," she said softly. "You've outgrown it." Suddenly she sat bolt upright. "And if you're too big for your dress, I'll bet that means you're too big for your boots, too. Am I right?"

I stood there, still half-out of the dress, and nodded. "Oh, Mom, what can we do?"

This was a double whammy. My green dress was a hand-me-down from my cousin, but she had given up skating, so I couldn't borrow anything more from her. How could I go to Regionals without a dress?

It's funny. A few days ago I'd been afraid of going

to Regionals. Now I was afraid I *wouldn't* get to go—and I felt disappointed rather than relieved. I hadn't realized just how much I wanted to be there despite everything that could go wrong. I guess what's worse than failing is not even getting the chance to fail.

"You can't help growing," Mom said, trying to calm me.

"But skating dresses are so expensive," I said, almost ready to cry. "Vanessa told us she spent a lot on her gold-star costume last year—you know, the one that lost all the beads."

"Well, I don't give up that easily—and you shouldn't either," Mom insisted. "I keep a little pin money for unexpected emergencies just like this. It should take care of at least part of the cost, and as for the rest," she smiled reassuringly, "well, we'll find a way. We always do, don't we?"

Mom is the real competitor in our family—only she does it with the family budget rather than on skates. I bet that she could teach even the coach a thing or two.

5

The Coin of Destiny

Mom got to enjoy being the center of attention the rest of that day and the next. Dad piled so many pillows and cushions behind her that she was practically sitting up rather than lying down. He would have spoiled her more, but the furnace was making more noise than ever while putting out less heat, so he spent a lot of time down in the basement, trying to nurse it back to health.

We each were wearing several sweaters against the growing cold, and unfortunately for Mom, my brothers decided to keep warm by taking care of her. In their typical fashion, they turned it into a competition, so if Mom asked for a cup of tea, she got three different flavors, which she had to take turns sipping so that she wouldn't hurt anyone's feelings.

If she wanted to watch television, my brothers fought over the remote, pressing the buttons insistently so that images flashed across the screen with headache-causing speed.

At Mom's suggestion, I'd borrowed a catalog of skating dresses from Anya so that we could pick one and order it in time for Regionals. I think she had hoped we two girls could spend some time alone selecting one, but my brothers turned it into yet another contest, each lobbying for a dress in his own team's colors. In the middle of a lecture from Rick about how green and gold were the best, there was a terrible groan from the basement, followed by a huge thud, as if an elephant had just collapsed.

Running to the cellar door, I shouted, "Dad, are you okay?"

To my relief, he trudged up the steps, his face streaked with dirt. "I'm fine," he said, hanging his head as if in mourning, "but that furnace and I have danced our last waltz together. I'm afraid that not even a truckload of duct tape can bring it back to life. It's finally time to get a new one." He knelt down next to the sofa where Mom was resting. Putting their heads together, they spoke in low, urgent whispers. They seemed almost ready to cry when they turned around.

"We need a family council," Dad said solemnly. I turned off the TV and joined my brothers on the rug.

Mom cleared her throat. "You know money's been tight lately. With this broken leg, I'll eventually get some disability income, but I won't be able to work at either of my jobs for a while. Which makes things even tighter than they already were."

Dad clasped his grimy hands. "And replacing the furnace is going to be a very expensive proposition. Your mom and I thought we could nurse it through one more season, but . . ."

"Macaroni and cheese, here we come," Rick sighed.

"Quiet, small fry," Perry said. "We'll make whatever sacrifices Mom and Dad say we need to make."

Mom and Dad exchanged glances, each of them reluctant to be the one to break the bad news to us. Finally, it was Mom who went on. "You know how your dad and I have always tried to let each of you live up to his or her potential."

"You've always been incredible that way," Skip reassured them, and the rest of us nodded.

"I've been trying and trying to make the figures work," Mom said, "but as you all know, we have two important things coming up—Mia's Regionals and Perry's tournament. Fees and travel are costly for both. And Mia has outgrown both her dress and her boots."

Dad blurted it out. "But now we have to get a new furnace, an expense we can't put off any longer. Which means that we can pay either for Perry to go to his tournament or for Mia to go to Regionals—but we can't do both."

"Can't we rough it like pioneers?" Rick asked, pantomiming chopping wood. "You know, burn logs in the fireplace?"

Dad shook his head. "The weather forecasters say that there's already a freeze coming. And that it's going to be an early and cold winter."

"There are going to be college scouts at Perry's tournament," I said in a small voice. This was going to be his big chance.

Perry, though, knew how much Regionals meant to me. "But you've dreamed about going to Regionals, and you've worked hard all year."

"Yeah," Skip agreed, "how many opportunities will Mia get? I hope it's lots, but maybe . . . well . . ." He let his shrug stand for the negative side.

"We know Perry can hold his own against any-one," Rick countered. "But up until now Mia's only skated against local competition. At Regionals, she'll have to go up against big-time skaters. She could be way out of her league. Maybe waiting a year would be good for her."

Perry and I studied each other uncomfortably. I knew that *he* knew how hard I've worked to be good enough to go to Regionals. But *I* knew how hard he's worked, too—and what the tournament means for him.

Suddenly, he clapped his hands together. "Well, there's only one thing to do."

I let my breath out slowly. I hadn't realized I'd been holding it. "Toss the Coin of Destiny," I said.

I'm not sure how other families handle difficult choices, but our family has been settling matters with Dad's magic thumb since Perry and Skip were small. I think it was Rick who came up with the name for it.

"Are you sure, both of you?" Mom asked quietly. "I wish we had a better way of settling this, but I'm at my wit's end as to how to do it."

"It's fairer than asking you to choose between us," Perry said.

I just nodded, not trusting my voice anymore.

Dad dug into his pocket and pulled out a quarter. "Heads or tails?" he asked me.

"Heads," I said.

With a flick of his thumb, he sent the coin tumbling end over end upward into the air. The reflected lamplight flickered from the sides, and I couldn't help thinking that my future rested on that one silly coin.

And then it was falling. When it landed on the carpet, it flipped over. It was tails.

Perry looked at me sadly. "I'm sorry, Sis. How about we make it two out of three?"

I couldn't help thinking that my future rested on that one silly coin.

My lip wanted to tremble, but I stopped it. If our parents have taught us one thing, it is to be good sports. "There's nothing to be sorry for. And no to two out of three. The risk was fifty-fifty, so the toss could have just as easily gone against you."

Perry understood me too well. "But I know what Regionals mean to you."

He was trying to be kind, but talking about it was only making the hurt worse. "And I know what the tournament means to you. It's . . . it's okay, Perry. Honestly, I'm happy for you."

"You've got guts, Sis," Skip said approvingly, looking at me with the same respect he would give to someone who had just taken one for the team.

Perry's head drooped. "But no glory." I think he was feeling almost as bad as I was that I had lost.

For his sake, I tried to keep my head up high. "I'm not giving up on my dreams," I said. "I'm just postponing them for a little while." At least, I hoped that was all it was, and that I would get another chance. When I felt the stinging at the corners of my eyes, I knew my own private Niagara Falls was coming on. "Now, if you'll excuse me," I murmured.

I had wanted to march out of there with dignity, but instead I wound up running from the room.

6

Family Hearts

About an hour later, I was still crying quietly into my pillow when I heard a tap at my door. "What is it?"

Skip's voice came muffled through the door. "I just thought you might want some hot chocolate to cheer—I mean, to *warm* you up."

"I don't feel like company now," I said.

Skip opened the door a crack so that the aroma could waft into the room. "But hot chocolate always makes you feel better."

I gave in. Dragging my sleeve across my eyes to wipe away any last tears, I sat up. "Sure, uh, thanks. Come in."

Behind Skip were Rick and Perry. Their large frames were even bulkier because of all the sweatshirts and sweaters they were wearing against the cold.

"We were out of the little marshmallows, but I found this big one in the back of the drawer." Skip held out the cup so that I could see a large, dented marshmallow floating on top of the full mug like a glacier on a chocolate sea. "It's kind of stale, but I figure it won't matter when it melts."

I wondered in what year the old, rock-hard marshmallow was going to do that.

"Go on, drink up," Skip urged.

I tried, but when I did, the huge marshmallow kept bumping my nose, so I could manage only a sip. "Thanks," I said.

"It's so cold that I thought you might like an extra blanket," Rick said as he deposited one at the foot of my bed. It had originally been decorated with the logo and colors of his favorite team, but over the years Mom had repaired it so often that there wasn't much left of the original blanket. It looked more like a patchwork quilt that had been handed down through generations.

Perry's hands were jammed in his pockets and he looked miserable. "I just wanted to tell you again that I'm really sorry."

I had to let him know that I wasn't holding any grudges. With my free hand, I opened the drawer of my nightstand and pulled out a deck of cards.

"You might have beaten me at the coin toss, but I bet your luck doesn't hold up at cards," I said.

He grinned. "Hearts?"

Setting down the cup, I nodded and began to shuffle the cards. "Merciless Mia is going to have you weeping and gnashing your teeth in no time." I jerked my head at Skip and Rick. "All three of you."

Despite my bragging, my head wasn't really into playing. Besides, I wound up getting the queen of spades. The aim of the game is to get as few points as possible, which means avoiding the hearts, each of which counts for one point, and the queen of spades, which equals all the hearts packed together. So now that I was stuck with her, I already had a whopping thirteen points. *Unless* . . . I glanced at my brothers.

Their foreheads were wrinkled as they each worked out the strategy for the cards in their hands. My heart started to race as a new thought bubbled up in my mind.

It requires a lot of luck and skill, but if you take all the hearts cards, along with the queen of spades, you can pull off a stunt that's called "shooting the moon." Then you can choose to deduct twenty-six points from your score or give each of your opponents twenty-six points instead.

I'd only managed to do that a couple of times against my cutthroat brothers, but hey, as my family always says, no guts, no glory, right?

Slyly, I pretended to be disgusted each time they dumped more hearts on me. When they finally understood what I was up to, it was too late. With growing excitement, I drew all the other hearts from them. It was with great satisfaction that I wrote a 26 under each of their names.

I might have been unlucky with the Coin of Destiny, but I was a genius with cards. I managed to shoot the moon in the next two games, with appropriate groans and lamentations from my brothers. I was trying my best not to gloat, because I'd never skunked them by seventy-eight points before, when suddenly it hit me. I'm good, but not *that* good.

I squinted at them suspiciously. "Have you guys been letting me win?"

Rick straightened indignantly. "I'm offended that you'd even suggest we'd throw a game. You're just too sharp for us tonight, Sis." Perry and Skip just nodded.

I glared at my three brothers until softhearted Skip cracked. "We didn't plan it, Sis," he said, scratching behind his ear guiltily. "It just sort of happened."

"I don't want cheap victories," I snapped.

"Which is why you get in over your head," Rick said. "Remember that time you got stuck on the monkey bars at the playground?"

"I was only five," I reminded him.

"All the more reason why you shouldn't have taken that dare from the other kids," Perry said.

They had heard me crying, stuck at the top of the monkey bars, and had gotten me down.

"And you're still getting in over your head," Rick said. "Don't get me wrong about your figure skating. I realize now that what you do is great—and you're good at it. But did you have to pick something where we can't help you anymore?"

"Yeah," Skip agreed, "do you know how frustrating that is? If you get into trouble during your routine, all we can do is sit on our hands."

"We're not used to feeling helpless," Rick agreed.

"Especially where you're concerned," Skip added.

"Enough," Perry said to our brothers. "Mia's got more guts than I'll ever have—than any of us has. I'd be scared out of my wits to be out there all by myself on the ice."

Skip winced. "Yeah, I'll only play sports that surround me with lots of teammates. I know if I make a mistake, they'll make up for it. But out there, in the middle of an empty rink, you're all on your own."

I knew their words were meant to support me, but I wished they hadn't reminded me of how lonely it can be out on the ice with everyone watching only me. *Not that it matters anyway, since now I'm not going to Regionals,* I thought.

"I smell chocolate," Dad said from the doorway as he sniffed the air. "Just the thing to warm someone up."

"Want me to make you a cup, too?" Skip offered.

Mom and her crutches came thumping up behind Dad and into the room. "That depends on if it's really chocolate or if it's mud," she teased.

Skip rubbed the back of his neck, embarrassed. "That was a long time ago when I played that trick on Mia."

Mom plucked a tissue from the box on my desk and wiped my upper lip. "You're off the hook, Skip. It's just a milk mustache this time."

"Mom and I came up to tell you again how sorry we are," Dad said. He was wearing a heavy jacket and a wool cap.

My parents were still looking sad and worried. "What for?" I asked. "You're the best parents anyone could want."

"Ahem." Skip cleared his throat and clinked a nail against the side of the cup.

I laughed. "And the best brothers, too." I began to gather up the cards. "And this time, let's play hearts for real. Want to join in?" I asked Mom and Dad as I scooted over on my bed to make room for Mom and her awkward white cast. Dad pulled my desk chair close.

Family Hearts

"It's been a long time since we had a six-handed tournament," Dad agreed.

Mom was already reaching for the deck to shuffle the cards.

7

Fairy Godmothers

At my next practice, with nothing to lose, I just tried to skate to the music. It was almost as if I felt every note in my body, and it made me all the sadder to realize that I wouldn't be able to perform at Regionals.

The coach grinned and nodded through it all, and when practice was over, she said excitedly, "You're finally getting it! That was the best you've done so far!" She broke off when she saw my face. "What's wrong, Mia?"

When I told Coach Schubert, she looked as upset as Mom and Dad had been. She skated away in a wide ragged circle before she looped back to me. "I wish I could buy your boots and dress for you," she said, "but if I did it for one of my students, I'd have to do it for all."

"Thank you, Coach Schubert, but that would be special treatment—and that wouldn't be fair," I said.

"You're right." The coach nodded her under-standing. "Still, I wish there was something I could do."

I thanked the coach for her concern and then left the rink as quickly as I could. I didn't want to break into tears in front of her. Later, all day at school, I moved like a zombie, and I still felt numb inside when I went home.

Even if I didn't feel very happy, I put on a cheerful face when I walked through our front door. I'd intended to do Mom's chores, but I could see that she'd finished a lot of them already, in spite of her leg. She is a wonderful mother but a terrible patient, so I scolded her about overdoing it.

"Enough, already!" Mom protested with a laugh. "Claire brought me lunch and did a few things to help out this afternoon." Claire is our next-door neighbor. "Now," she stopped to yawn, "if you're done lecturing me, I think I'll take a snooze."

I was glad that I could get straight to my homework and keep busy. I didn't have a moment to think about my lost opportunity until I had finished all my assignments.

When I went back downstairs, Mom was still napping on the sofa, so I tucked a blanket around her— even though she was wearing a scarf and a coat. It was colder than ever in the house and we weren't scheduled to get our new furnace until tomorrow.

Bundling up even more, I left Mom a note and went down to the pond.

The cold, sunny weather had brought the color out in the trees, and I felt as if I were walking through a tunnel of bright red, gold, and orange tiles. The air was still, so the water was calm, reflecting the colors of the grove and the blue sky above.

The surface was so smooth, it might have been ice—and I wished it were. Skating on the pond always makes me feel better. It's my true home ice.

I brushed some leaves off a log and sat down, remembering all the hockey games my family had played here. Life was a lot simpler when my brothers and I were younger and the pond was the center of our world. There were no tournaments, no Regionals, no fees, and no disappointments—just skating and playing.

I sat there for a long time, ignoring the chill that started to creep through my jacket. Suddenly I heard the muffled strains of *Swan Lake* from inside my pocket. Rick had downloaded a section as the ring tone on my cell phone. I made a note to myself to ask him to change it to something less painful.

"Mia?" Mom's voice came through the phone. "Where are you? You've got visitors."

Puzzled, I said, "I'm at the pond. I left you a note on the table. But who's here?"

"I'll send them down to you," Mom said.

I started walking back up the path and ran into Bob and Nelda before they had come a third of the way. "Look at this," Nelda said as she took a big whiff of fresh, cold air. "I feel as if I've walked right into the middle of a greeting card."

Bob is happier with machines than he seemed to be with Mother Nature. "Humph," he snorted, "it would take some clearing up out here if you wanted to bring the Beast here to sweep the pond." "The Beast" is Bob's nickname for the Lucerne's old ice-resurfacing machine, and he tends it as if it were his baby. "But we didn't come here to commune with the Earth, did we?" he asked, nudging Nelda.

"No, we most definitely did not." Nelda tore her gaze from the trees and gave me a grin that Zuzu might have worn if she'd found a giant box of chocolate-covered nuts. "When the coach told us about your circumstances . . . well, we all thought it'd be a waste if you didn't get a chance to go to Regionals."

Bob shifted uncomfortably. Give him a micro-phone in the sound booth at the rink and he can talk all day, but he isn't used to giving speeches in person. "Mia, if you're not *skating* at the Lucerne, you're helping out there, so you spend almost as much time there as the staff." He cleared his throat. "We've come to think of you as one of the gang, so"—he took a plastic bag from behind his back and held it out to me—"Mona and I and the whole gang all chipped in to get you these."

I reached out my hand eagerly but then stopped. "I . . . I'm sorry, but I can't take it."

"You'd take help from your family, right?" Bob argued. "Well, we're like your family, aren't we?"

"Sure, but . . ." My fingers were itching to take the bag, but I still held back.

"We already asked your mom, and she said it was all right," Bob said.

When I opened the sack, I took out a pair of boots. "You got me new ones!"

"Technically, they're a used pair, but they've hardly been worn," Bob explained. "Mona must have called up every shop in six counties, and then she drove over to pick them up personally."

I ran my hand over the leather, which felt as smooth as if the boots had just come from the factory. It took me a moment to find my voice. "I don't know how to thank you."

Bob pointed at the blades with the guards he held in his hand. "I've been saving those to give you. They're the top of the line, with very little wear on them. And I sharpened them special for you."

Nelda held out another plastic sack. This one had Zuzu's face on it. "And here's my latest pattern for a skating dress, some new fabrics, and some special trims and embellishments that I think will go great with it. I believe in helping those who help themselves." She grabbed my free hand and pressed the sack into it. "And don't argue. Take it. Consider it payment from Zuzu for all the publicity you got her. And actually, you'd be doing me a favor if you would try it out. Test it, sort of. See if it's a good pattern."

Bob nodded encouragingly. "Yessir, Mia, you're going from squirrel to guinea pig."

Because of them, my miserable day had turned right-side up again. I couldn't believe it! I reached out and hugged both of them, thanking them over and over.

Nelda gave a snuffle and wiped her eyes. "Well, I shouldn't keep Zuzu waiting. She's got that new set of ads to shoot, and I ought to be there."

"And the Beast was coughing this morning, so I ought to see what's wrong," Bob said with a wave.

I walked them back to their cars, thanked them a few dozen more times, and then went inside the house where Mom was waiting. Together we examined the contents of Nelda's bag. The pattern was for one of the prettiest skating dresses I'd ever seen, and when we took the silvery fabric from the bag, it shimmered in our hands.

"Do you know how much this stuff costs?" Mom gasped.

"Lots?" I asked.

Mom took the trims and decorations from the bag and laid them across her lap. "Let's just say that when Zuzu thanks you, she *really* thanks you."

I looked again at the fancy material. Crooked seams and puckered fabric would ruin even the best dress design. "Um, do you think you can handle it, Mom?" I asked, remembering the Halloween costume disaster.

"It's so beautiful that it makes me nervous to even *think* of cutting it. And I don't know how I can sit at the sewing machine with this cast. But maybe you can help me with it," she said. "You know how to sew now."

"But I'm just a beginner. Sort of like a Twinkle, only in sewing," I pointed out. "Where do we start?"

We gazed helplessly at Nelda's gift, spread out in front of us on the coffee table. "Such a lovely design and material," Mom said, running her fingers wonderingly over the fabric. "It'd be a waste not to use them, and yet it would be such a waste to botch sewing them."

"Hey, no guts, no glory," I said, reminding her of the family motto.

But each of us was so afraid to attempt it that we just sat there holding the material. We might have been sitting there all afternoon if Coach Schubert hadn't rung the doorbell.

"I just came by to see how things were going," she explained. "How's your leg, Eve?" Then she saw the gifts from Nelda and Bob. "Is this what Nelda brought? She asked me if I thought you'd accept it, and I told her it was a possibility." Her eyes shone as she inspected Nelda's gift. "Wonderful! She's outdone herself with the design. And the material! It's so lovely, and such a perfect color for you, Mia. I can't wait to see it when it's finished."

"Neither can I," Mom said gloomily.

"Is something wrong?" the coach asked, puzzled.

Mom cleared her throat uncomfortably. "I haven't always had the greatest success sewing stretch fabrics."

"It can be tricky," the coach acknowledged, and then she turned her eyes to me.

I shook my head. "I'm still pretty new at sewing."

"No wonder you both looked so down when I came in." The coach rubbed her chin thoughtfully. "This is like giving a hungry person a can of ravioli and no can opener." She started to take off her jacket and then thought better of it in our chilly house. "Maybe I can help. I can't buy a dress for you. However, there's nothing wrong with helping you make one."

"You sew, too?" Mom blurted out in amazement.

"I wouldn't have had skating costumes if I hadn't learned how. My family never had a lot of money." She held up her hand. "When I was a kid, I used to have bandages on all my fingers at first. I've got the photos to prove it. But I think the most painful part was having the other skaters make fun of my clothes while I was learning how to sew my dresses."

I let that sink in. "If it was that hard, did you ever feel like quitting?"

"It was even harder on my family," the coach confessed, "but there was never a question of quitting. My father always used to say that it takes a lot of work to get anything of real value. But then it's all the sweeter when you attain it."

Mom's sewing machine was set up on a small table in the corner of the living room. The coach took some measurements and then sat down and made adjustments to the machine. "I warn you, though, Mia," the coach said, "this is going to cost you. I'm going to expect you to work twice as hard at practice from now on."

I felt a wave of excitement surge through me now

that I had hope again. "That's just what I plan to do," I promised. "You don't throw away a second chance."

"I thought you'd say that," she said approvingly.

It was like magic watching the dress take shape under the coach's skillful hands, and while she cut and sewed, we eagerly discussed my routine. I had performed it so often that by now we'd developed our own shorthand method of talking about each element, so it was almost like a secret code.

The coach and I were lost in our own little world when Mom interrupted. "I'm a terrible host. Can I get either of you anything?"

That was the last thing she should be doing with a broken leg. "Please, Mom. I'll do it. You take it easy," I urged.

"But you're busy, and I'm not doing anything anyway," she said.

At first, I couldn't understand why she was frowning. After all, the coach was sewing the dress for us so that I'd be able to go to Regionals.

"I'm sorry," the coach apologized to Mom. "We've been rude, talking skating like that."

"No, please don't mind me," Mom said. "You can help Mia with this, and I can't."

When I thought about it, I guess we *had* sort of

left Mom out of the conversation.

The coach glanced at me. "I hope you won't be disappointed, but I can only help you with the sewing machine part." She nodded at everything that was still spread across the coffee table. "It's all those things that will really make the dress, and I'm not good with a needle and thread. My mother and aunt used to finish all my skating outfits for me."

Mom perked up. "I'm much better with a needle and thread than I am on the machine."

"Then maybe you and Mia should start thinking about the next step," the coach suggested. "Anyway, I should focus on the dress instead of babbling."

Mom looked at the coach skeptically, as if she suspected that the coach was as skillful with hand sewing as she was with a machine, but she was glad of the excuse, and so was I.

It was fun to plan out the rest of the dress and the hair accessory with Mom, and as we discussed it all, Mom was always diplomatic enough to ask the coach's opinion. And the coach was just as polite, deferring to Mom's judgment.

The two of them could have given lessons to the United Nations about getting along.

8

The Oakville Arms

Mom's leg was healing well, so the doctor replaced her bulky and heavy cast with a lightweight fiberglass one just before we left for Regionals. Mom said it was more comfortable, and I could see that she was getting around more easily. We rode up with Anya and her mother in their car, the moms in the front and Anya and I in the back. Even with the competition looming ahead of me, it still felt like a holiday to be together with both Mom and my friends.

When I travel with my brothers to hockey tournaments in faraway cities, we always stay at inexpensive motels that are nothing like the Oakville Arms. At twelve stories, the hotel towered above the surrounding buildings, and it actually had a chandelier in the lobby!

The lobby was packed with skaters of all levels and their families and coaches. Some of the skaters were even younger than we were. Adding to the hubbub were fans snapping pictures.

Anya, her mother, and I tried to protect Mom as we threaded our way through the mob and got into line at the reservation desk.

Back home, I'd felt so important to be competing at Regionals, but now that I was here, I felt as small and insignificant as a candle trying to compete with the sun. Instinctively, Anya and I drew close together until we were shoulder to shoulder.

"Welcome to the pressure cooker," Chad said to Anya. He and Izumi had sneaked up on us in the mob.

"There are so many people!" Anya said, looking dazed.

"You'll get used to it," Izumi said with a smile.

"Chad, Izumi," a woman said, "could I have a few words with you for my fanzine?"

I turned to see a middle-aged woman with a small digital voice recorder.

"You'll get used to this, too." Chad winked.

"Of course," Izumi said politely to the woman, "but may we introduce you to our clubmates first? This is Anya Sorokowski and Mia St. Clair." She indicated the woman. "Anya, Mia, this is Yvette Polk, figure skating's number one fan."

Chad added, "This is their first Regionals, and they're definitely skaters to watch."

Ms. Polk nodded to us as she said, "Pleased to meet you."

As Ms. Polk led Izumi and Chad away to find a quiet corner, I just stood there in a glow, happy that they had treated Anya and me as equals.

When some bright lights went on, I noticed the television reporter Lillian Chin interviewing Coach Schubert. I guess our television station had decided to follow the doings of our local Olympic celebrity.

"I wish Vanessa's father could see this," I said to Anya.

"Speak of the deviled egg." Anya jerked her head toward the counter.

Mr. Knowles was there, arguing in turn with the clerk at the desk and with someone on his cell phone. "My secretary made this reservation months ago," he said to the clerk and then, as the clerk started to reply, Mr. Knowles put up an index finger so that he could talk on the phone. "Yes, I know I promised, but it will have to wait until next week." He winced now and then as he listened to the caller's response.

Vanessa sat on a suitcase nearby, drumming her heels against the floor impatiently. "Daddy, make that clerk give us our room."

"Excuse . . . excuse . . . excuse me." It took a few moments before Mr. Knowles could get a word in edgewise with his caller. Then, still keeping the phone to his ear, he faced the clerk again. "Look, forget the suite. We'll take anything you've got."

The clerk raised his hands. "I'm sorry, sir, but we don't have even a supply closet to spare. The hotel's all booked up."

Mr. Knowles gestured for the clerk to wait while he talked to his caller once more. "You can hardly expect my daughter to sleep on a sofa in the lobby. No, my wife *isn't* here. She got called away on business. She won't be back until later."

Mom glanced at Mrs. Sorokowski, who nodded, and then she turned to us and raised an eyebrow. "I bet we could fit a cot into our room, girls."

I would sooner have shared a room with a porcupine than with Vanessa, and from Anya's expression, so would she.

"Coach Schubert said that we're all teammates," I reminded Anya weakly, hoping that she would object.

She only sighed. "And Chad and Izumi just treated us as teammates."

"I guess it's okay," I said to Mom.

Mom could move pretty fast on her crutches now, and she started forward with Mrs. Sorokowski's hotel confirmation in her hand. "Excuse me. Emergency. Invalid coming through . . . No need to get huffy with me, lady! I'm not taking your spot in line—I'm just trying to help someone out," she said as she made her way to the front of the line, where Mr. Knowles was still trying to argue simultaneously with his caller and the clerk.

"Hello," Mom said to Mr. Knowles. "I'm Eve St. Clair, and we're in Vanessa's skating club. Assuming that *we* have a room, Vanessa's welcome to stay with us."

Relieved, Mr. Knowles lowered his cell phone. "Yes, I remember you, Ms. St. Clair. How do you do? That's very kind."

To my annoyance, Vanessa looked as if she would rather sleep on a lobby sofa than in the same room with us. Well, at least we had *one* thing in common.

Vanessa nearly tipped her suitcase over when she jumped to her feet. "If you have a room for them, you must have something for us."

"I told you, *little girl*"—the clerk gritted his teeth as he emphasized the last two words—"I don't have a thing." He glanced at the confirmation number on Mrs. Sorokowski's receipt. After his fingers deftly danced over the keyboard, he said, "However, we do have a room for *you*, madam. And we can put in a cot for *her*." His eyes flicked toward Vanessa as if she were the family curse.

Her guilty father made a point of not looking at

his daughter. "Thank you so much," he said to Mom, handing her a small white business card. "Both my office and cell numbers are there, and here's my wife's cell number, in case you need to reach us. I'll try to check in later." He wrote quickly on the back of the card. Then he wheeled around to Vanessa and pecked her cheek. "Good-bye, kitten. Be good. I'll be back in time for your program."

"Dad-dee!" She packed more emotion into that one word than Mayor Chuck did into a whole speech.

Mr. Knowles winced, but he held firm. "I'm sorry, kitten. But what can I do? I'll be back as soon as I can—and with something extra nice for you." Snatching up his bag, he began to weave his way through the crowd as he spoke again into his cell phone. "Yes, I'm leaving right now."

As he left, Vanessa stared after him in shock and disbelief.

9

Snug as Two Bugs in a Rug

After we finished checking in and got our keys, we headed to the elevator. The ceiling and the sides had wood paneling, and Anya and I couldn't resist poking each other and gazing up at the elevator's crystal mini-chandelier because neither of us had ever seen anything like it. When we got to the room, she and I immediately went to the window to admire the view.

"What a dump." Vanessa frowned in disgust.

Up until then, Anya and I had been enjoying our first fancy hotel. I glanced at Anya now, and she raised and lowered her shoulders resignedly. It would have been nice to have been able to enjoy this moment with her, but we couldn't talk about it without having Vanessa think we were hicks.

Vanessa prodded one of the double beds. "I'll take this one." She plopped onto the bed.

Mom turned on her crutches to look at Anya's mother. "Is that all right with you, Marie, or do you and Anya prefer that bed? I think that Mia should share with Vanessa, and then I'll take the cot. With this cast, it'll be easier for me to sleep by myself."

I would rather have slept on the floor than with the divine Miss V. However, Mom insisted—to Vanessa's and my mutual distress.

Vanessa, of course, tried to hog most of the bureau and the hangers in the closet, so she looked as if she was ready to cry when Mom and Mrs. Sorokowski insisted we share everything equally. I don't think Vanessa's used to having anyone say no to her.

When she started to take her stuff out of her suitcase, Anya and I stopped our own unpacking to watch. Vanessa had clothes and toiletries that I'd only seen advertised in slick, expensive magazines, and the closest I got to the perfume she pulled out of her bag was rubbing a sampler page on my wrist. Even Mom and Mrs. Sorokowski paused. When Vanessa became aware that she had an audience, she began a running commentary. "And this top came from a couturier in Paris. It's a one-of-a-kind," she said as she hung it up.

"Ah, the City of Lights is so lovely," Mrs. Sorokowski sighed. "What did you like best about it?"

"Oh, I didn't get to go." Vanessa hesitated. "My mother brought the top back for me. It was a quick trip, so she couldn't take me. And . . . and . . . ," Vanessa shook her head, "I was too busy training, anyway."

She lifted out a silky skirt next. "Daddy got this

one for me in Montreal."

It was the same thing with all the rest of the contents of her suitcase. Each item was a souvenir given to Vanessa by her parents after a business trip without her. I bet that her clothes have traveled more than Vanessa has.

When the rest of us had put away our things, Mom suggested we call our families. When Vanessa took out her cell phone, she brightened, telling us that she had a message from her mother. However, her face quickly fell again. Her mother, she soon informed us, was no longer sure she could even get to Regionals. And when Vanessa tried to reach her father, she was only able to leave a message.

Anya and Mrs. Sorokowski called Anya's sister and father on their cell phone. Mrs. Sorokowski had cooked and frozen meals for them, and even though she clearly had left instructions, she went over the order in which each thing should be thawed and for how long.

Bored, Vanessa began flipping through the pages of a magazine she had found in the room.

As Mrs. Sorokowski reviewed the cooking schedule, I whispered to Mom, "Dr. Sorokowski teaches physics at the college. Couldn't he figure it out?"

"She just wants to fuss over them a little bit and

let them know she cares," Mom explained.

Later, Mom did the same sort of thing when we called home. When it was my turn to talk, all three of my brothers tried to speak to me simultaneously—which meant they were shouting into the receiver. Naturally, my voice got louder in response—loud enough that Vanessa looked up from her magazine curiously.

"And don't worry, Sis," Perry assured me, "we'll take good care of your animals."

"I don't have any pets," I pointed out . . . but I did have stuffed animals. "Did you go into my room? Didn't you see the no-trespassing sign?"

"Ohhh, is *that* what you wrote?" Perry asked.

"Your handwriting's terrible, Mia," Rick yelled.

"You harm one fiber on them, and I'll . . ." I began. Mom made a gesture for me to give her the telephone again. But I shook my head. I'd handle my brothers on my own. "Perry, I will let everyone know who you had a crush on last summer. Rick, I will broadcast to your school and team the disgusting things you used to do and blame on your imaginary friend, Mr. Sniggles. And Skip—"

"We'll put them back! We'll put them back," Skip promised frantically.

"And the three of you will stay out of my room

from now on, unless invited back in," I said firmly.

I was grinning as I handed the telephone back to my mother.

"And I know even more embarrassing dirt about you boys than your sister does," Mom warned them. "I realize it's too much to expect you to actually be *gentlemen* while we're gone, but I want you to try to approximate trained apes, at least. Got it?" From her satisfied expression when she hung up, I could see that she felt she had done her job in keeping the boys in line.

"So give with the dish," I said eagerly. "What else did they do?"

Mom patted me on the head. "Down, girl. For every secret I tell you, I'd have to tell them a secret about their little sister. A mother has to be fair, you know."

"Where does it say that in the Mommy Manual?" I grumbled.

Mom plugged the cell phone into the charger and set it on the nightstand. "On page twenty-five. It's in big, bold type."

I was about to remind her that we girls have to stick together when I saw Vanessa staring at us, looking as if we had just stepped out of a flying saucer. I guess she and her mother don't have fun with each other this way. Well, whenever I see Mrs. Knowles, every hair looks as if it were sprayed in place. She's very elegant, but she isn't the sort of person I would tease, either, if she were my mother.

And Vanessa looked even more puzzled when, during dinner in a restaurant, Anya and I kept snagging tidbits from our mothers' plates and from each other. Vanessa didn't seem to understand that it was just another game among us.

That made me wonder just what Vanessa actually does with her parents, but maybe it's like this afternoon—maybe they are just so busy making money that they don't have much time for her. I guess they buy her expensive presents to make up for not being around.

That evening, I put on Perry's lucky jersey, which he had loaned to me temporarily. I was even more touched that he had thought to wash it for me first. It was so big that I could wear it like a nightgown. As we watched television and I snuggled up against Mom and Anya cuddled against her mother, I actually felt sorry for Vanessa, who sat by herself, painting her nails.

Even though Vanessa seems to get everything she asks for, and we St. Clairs seem to struggle for everything we get, I don't think I would trade places with her. I'd much rather have Mom next to me than have a whole bunch of things in a suitcase. I think that, at that moment, Vanessa would rather have had a mother like mine, too.

And later that night, I was *sure* that I didn't want to trade places with Vanessa. I woke when I felt her stirring in the bed. As I lay there listening to everyone else sleeping softly, I heard an odd, muffled sound.

I rolled over to check on Vanessa. There was enough light from the street to see her shoulders shaking as she pressed her face into the pillow.

Worried, I sat up and leaned over her. "Are you okay?" I asked quietly.

When she lifted her face from the pillow, I saw that her eyes were puffy and her pillow was damp from what must have been her tears. "None of your business," she snapped.

"If you're feeling sick, I'll wake Mom," I offered.

"Just leave me alone," she said, and she hid her face back in her pillow.

She seemed so miserable, though, that I couldn't do that. "You can talk to me. I'm on my own a lot. My mom's usually busy with work, just like yours is. If she hadn't broken her leg, she never would have been able to come for the whole trip."

Vanessa's voice came stifled from the pillow. "You certainly get along well enough when you *are* together."

"Yeah, but your dad will be back soon. And I bet your mom will make it, too," I whispered.

"Unless something *important* comes up," she insisted. "And it usually does."

"But this is Regionals," I said in disbelief.

She turned her head so that she could give me a superior look. "Grow up. Not all parents are like yours. Mine always let me down in the end."

"That's not true," I insisted.

"How would you know?" she snapped at me again. She saw the pity in my eyes and glanced away. "If I didn't have skating," she confessed in a softer tone,

Snug as Two Bugs in a Rug

"I don't know what I would do."

I hadn't realized how lonely Vanessa must be. She's an only child, so if she doesn't trust her parents, she really has no family to depend on. And when I thought about it, the only person Vanessa hangs around with is Gemma, and Gemma is sort of a mirror image of Vanessa.

They're both spoiled, and they show it. And the only thing they do together, besides showing off their expensive stuff, is make fun of other people. It's no wonder that no one else wants to be around them. Maybe if they had a choice, they wouldn't be with each other either.

I was willing to bet that even when Vanessa is with Gemma, she still feels as lonely as if she were by herself.

Maybe that's why she acts high-and-mighty—so people won't know how she really feels inside.

10

Practice

The next day we went to practice at the arena where the competitions would take place.

The arena itself looked like a huge half-cylinder buried on its side. Outside, a marquee over the entrance welcomed the regional skaters, and inside, the ceiling was so high that the bright lights hung like miniature suns. Orange seats rose up on all sides, like the scales of a plastic crocodile.

Though it was early in the morning, there was already a skater on the ice, practicing her routine under her coach's watchful eye. Other skaters and coaches sat near the rink, chatting while they waited their turns. Coach Schubert was with them, and when she saw us, she waved. I was surprised, though, to see another fifty or so people scattered around the stands. I motioned to the other folks sprinkled about the seats. "Who are they?"

Vanessa dumped her bag down on a seat and pointed to a small group sitting nearby. "Skating fans," she said. "They're here to see the new talent, especially her." She pointed to a tall girl about our age with curly brown hair pulled back off her face. "Paige is from the Belmont Skating Club."

If there is a powerhouse skating club in the area, the Belmont is it.

"I hear the Belmont has two rinks," Anya said in awe.

"They've sent a lot of senior-level skaters to Nationals," Vanessa explained, "and the best in our group level is Paige Clement. During the skating season, she's at a different competition every weekend. The list of the stuff she's done is as long as my arm." She nodded at a blonde girl with short hair next to Paige and a girl with long black hair. "And they've got lists almost as long." They were all wearing jackets dotted with pins.

For a moment, I felt nervous because they were exactly the kind of competition Rick had been afraid of, but Vanessa started down the steps.

"Where are you going?" Mrs. Sorokowski asked.

Vanessa glanced at Paige. "To say hello, of course."

Anya hesitated, unsure if we should go with Vanessa, but Vanessa waved at her to stay put. "We've already met, but they don't know you." She made it sound as if she belonged to an exclusive club and we didn't.

Mom dug a bag of dried apple snacks from her backpack and ripped it open. "Here, girls," she said, handing it around.

Mrs. Sorokowski rummaged around some more in Mom's backpack, rejecting each item that she found in there. "Healthy. Pah, healthy. *Healthy.*" She looked up, disappointed. "No chips?"

"I warned Mrs. St. Clair about your blood pressure," Anya explained.

Mrs. Sorokowski's eyes narrowed. "And who told you?"

"Dad told me." Anya shrugged. "I want you around for a long time."

"We all do, Marie," Mom said.

With a grunt, Mrs. Sorokowski took a handful of snacks and began crunching them, but she didn't look very happy about it. "I know that junk food's not good for me, but I find that things always taste better with salt and barbecue sauce . . . although I should set a better example for my daughter!"

We were about a dozen rows back, so we could hear Vanessa as she greeted the other skaters. "Hi, Paige."

"Oh, very well, what's your name?" Paige sighed as she held out her palm—and then seemed surprised when Vanessa shook her hand.

"Vanessa Knowles," Vanessa said. "We met at the Springfield Invitational last year."

Paige extricated her hand from Vanessa's grasp and kept her palm extended in the same way as before. I realized that she hadn't been reaching out to shake Vanessa's hand but to take a paper for an autograph. "So who do you want me to sign my name for this time?"

"No one. We competed against one another," Vanessa said indignantly.

Paige, though, just looked blank.

"You know." Vanessa was sounding desperate now. "I'm from the Lucerne."

"Sorry. I meet a lot of skaters." Paige glanced at her friends, but they both shook their heads as if they couldn't remember Vanessa, either.

"My parents are pretty busy, so I don't get to go to as many places as I'd like," Vanessa said and then hurriedly rattled off the half-dozen invitationals that she had been at.

She impressed me, but not Paige or her friends. "It's nice to know you've done so well training at such a little club," the blonde girl said snottily.

"Anyway, here's what I heard about Justin," the

third girl said, turning away from Vanessa to Paige and the blonde girl.

Though their backs were to her now, Vanessa stood there, peering over their shoulders and trying to act as if they were including her in their conversation.

"Poor Vanessa," Mom said to me in a quiet voice. "She's been a big frog in a little pond. But now she's finding out that there are bigger ponds with bigger frogs."

It was sort of what Coach Schubert had warned us about, and what my brothers had also been afraid of.

It was a scary thought, and even scarier to go near the big frogs, but Vanessa seemed so miserable that I couldn't leave her there. I took the steps two at a time until I could reach out and tap her on the shoulder. "Vanessa, I'm sorry to bother you, but my mom has something she needs to ask you."

Now that I was closer, I could see that the pins the girls were wearing were souvenirs of the many competitions and invitationals that they had been to. Compared to them, with all their experiences, I felt like a beginning Twinkle.

"Oh . . . uh . . . sure," Vanessa said to me and then announced to Paige and her friends, "Well, bye. I've got to go now."

However, they didn't acknowledge her—if they

even heard her at all.

Vanessa stared down at the steps as we climbed upward. "So what did your mom want to ask me?"

"Do you want something to nibble on?" I asked. "I'm warning you, though, the snacks Mom brought are all healthy. I mean, what kind of self-respecting snack is *good* for you?"

"You called me away for that?" she demanded, annoyed.

I just shrugged.

She glanced back at Paige and her friends and then mumbled, "You didn't have to bother. I was about to leave anyway."

"Well, you got to do it earlier," I snapped, annoyed at her ingratitude.

I had the first practice session of our group, and Paige Clement's slot was right before mine. I changed in the locker rooms and when I came back, I found that Mom and the others had moved down to the front row with Coach Schubert. At one end of the rink, leaning against the wall, was Paige's coach, Sam McManus. He's a chubby man whose trademark look is a tweed coat and a fedora hat, which he waved for emphasis as he shouted instructions at Paige.

If I wanted an autograph from anyone here besides Coach Schubert, it would be from Coach McManus. In his long career, he's trained a lot of skaters who have made it to Nationals and to the Olympics. Because of his reputation, elite skaters come from all around the country to train with him at the Belmont.

And Paige certainly belonged at the top of the class. I could see why she had placed well at so many competitions. She was good—very good. She skated fast and with confidence and grace, and she had the power to propel herself high up from the ice. Honestly, I thought she should have been skating at the next level rather than at ours. There were actually a dozen fans recording her every move on their camcorders.

"She's even better than the last time I saw her," Vanessa said to Anya and me in awe. "How are we going to beat someone like her?"

Her question made me wonder if Vanessa had ever had to fight for anything in her whole life. Her parents seem to buy her whatever she wants, but a place on the podium is one thing their money can't get for her. I don't think she knows how to handle a situation as frustrating as that.

"So we should give up before we even get onto the ice, and just hand her first place?" I demanded. "Paige gets the same two minutes that we do to impress the judges." I remembered the conversation I'd had with Coach Schubert when the coach was sewing my costume. "Sure, it's going to be hard, but that's what makes it so worthwhile when you win. I almost never beat my brothers, but once in a while I do, and then I feel on top of the world."

"Until the next time they beat you," Anya pointed out.

I grinned. "But if I won once, I know that I can win again."

"You're crazy," Vanessa declared.

Because of my brothers, competing seems as natural to me as breathing. But Vanessa has grown up an only child, and a pretty lonely one, since her parents seem constantly busy. I might as well have been talking Martian to her.

Anya began to jiggle her knee nervously. "I'll just be happy if I don't fall."

I remembered my day as Zuzu the Squirrel. There had been moments when I hadn't felt like *Mia* but actually like Zuzu herself—and those were the times when I'd been best at acting like a squirrel. "So stop being Anya Sorokowski when you're out there. If you fall, it's not the real Anya Sorokowski, but Anya the Skater. So think Anya the Skater, act Anya the Skater, be Anya the Skater."

Mom glanced at her watch and then said to me, "It's time for your practice, honey."

Down by the wall, Coach McManus was signaling Paige to get off the rink.

"But I'd like to get that sequence near the start down pat," Paige said to her coach, and then she saw me standing by the doorway onto the ice. "You understand, don't you?" Without waiting for me to say anything, she started on her routine again, although this time without the music.

"No, it's someone else's turn," Coach McManus called out and gestured urgently with his hat for her to leave the ice.

"But she doesn't mind," Paige protested.

I gathered up my courage. "Actually, I do."

Paige shot me a dirty look as she skated to Coach McManus's end of the rink. Her coach was so mad at her that he hardly let her get off the ice and through the other doorway before he started to scold her.

"Things like this are going to happen," Coach Schubert advised me as she put out her hand to take my skate guards, "so don't let it get to you. You've been a regular ball of fire during your last few practices at home. Let me see that same skater now."

As I skated out onto the ice, I couldn't help glancing toward Paige. I couldn't hear Coach McManus, but his face had become red and he was wagging his index finger at her. Paige stood there, still in her skates, head bent but turned so that she could stare at me resentfully, as if it were my fault that her coach was so mad.

Suddenly he stopped talking to Paige and pulled out his cell phone. It must have been an urgent call, because he looked anxious as he quickly climbed up the stairs.

"Concentrate!" Coach Schubert called.

I had barely started my routine when I saw someone aiming his camcorder not at me but at the far end of the rink. Twisting my head, I saw that Paige was on the ice and clowning to my music! As she made faces, she flailed her arms as if she were about to fall, narrowly keeping her balance.

Other fans were digging out their camcorders. I was so busy watching them and her that I tripped over my own feet. As I sprawled on the ice, I saw Paige leaping up in a double lutz that was higher, faster, and better than any I had ever done.

Bravo, Mia!

"Get up!" Coach Schubert ordered sharply. "You're on an ice rink, not a bed. Never mind her. Just focus!"

As I rose to my feet, I could feel myself growing angry—not at Paige but at myself. I wouldn't let my brothers get away with something like that, so why was I letting some stranger do it? It was time to follow my own advice to Anya and Vanessa. Even if my brothers are better than I am at most things, I haven't given up against them. And I couldn't do that now.

I picked up my routine to match the music. I had another double lutz ahead of me, and this time when I launched myself from the ice, I found myself spinning through the air perfectly. I'd never been so high, and when I landed, I felt Bob's specially sharpened blade bite the ice perfectly.

That's when I glimpsed one of the fans switching her camcorder over to me. And that was a triumph in itself.

When the music ended, Coach Schubert waved me over, and as I skated toward her, I heard Coach McManus bellow, "Paige, what do you think you're doing?!" I saw him galloping down the stairs, waving his hat over his head like a flag. "You need to apologize immediately."

*I wouldn't let my brothers get away with something like that,
so why was I letting some stranger do it?*

Paige seemed to shrink. "I'm sorry," she called. "I lost my temper."

This time, Coach McManus made Paige leave the arena entirely.

In the meantime, Coach Schubert was waiting for me with folded arms. "So what do you do if someone tops your jump?"

"You don't worry about it. You just focus on your own program and do your best," I said without hesitating. "Maybe you'll even top theirs."

Coach Schubert nodded approvingly. "Right, because when you're focused, you *will* do your best. That's how you use the competition to improve. Remember that the next time you meet Paige."

That was going to be a lot sooner than I wanted.

11

The Skaters

On the day of our event, I thought there might be fifty people in the arena, as there had been at the practice, but there were triple that number instead. Some of them were family, but Vanessa said some of them were fans.

Anya's father and little sister, Alexandra, had driven up that morning, and they waved a homemade sign at Anya. But Vanessa's parents were nowhere to be seen—though she looked all around for them. She tried to pretend it didn't matter, but from her frown I knew that it did.

There was no sign of Dad or my brothers, and that worried me. "I hope they didn't have an accident on the way here," I said to Mom.

"I'm sure they're just fine," Mom assured me and then hobbled over on her crutches to sit with the Sorokowskis in the stands. "Come sit with us."

We skated in groups of six, and by chance

Bravo, Mia!

Vanessa and Anya were in the third group while I was in the last group with my old buddy, Paige. So as their turns approached, I went along with Anya, Vanessa, and the coach to the roped-off waiting area by the door to the ice. Only skaters and coaches are allowed there, and it gave me a little thrill to show my official skater's credential badge to the guard. I was planning to keep it as a special souvenir of the day.

In the locker room at the rear of the waiting area, I helped Anya and Vanessa change and then accompanied them back toward the doorway.

I surveyed the stands again, but Vanessa kept her eyes on the rink as if that were her whole world now. "Don't bother," she said resignedly to me. "They won't be here."

Poor Vanessa. I hoped that her parents *would* show up soon.

Standing next to us, Anya was getting more nervous with each passing moment. I was trying to encourage her when I saw some people pointing at us. Since Anya and Vanessa were the ones in skates, I thought they must be the ones attracting attention. "Look. Word must have spread about you two," I said.

Vanessa glanced at me sideways. "Don't be a dope. *You're* the one they're curious about. They heard about your run-in with Paige yesterday."

"How?" I asked dumbly.

"Skating gossip moves with the speed of light, and juicy stuff even faster," Vanessa said. "And the way those things get twisted in the telling, they're probably saying that you were the one throwing a tantrum."

I felt my stomach do flip-flops. I had thought that yesterday had been like a disagreement at a play-ground: However important it might seem at the time, everyone forgets about it as soon as they go home. But now it seemed I had become The Girl Who Was Going to Be Steamrolled Over by Paige the Rising Superstar.

For a moment, I could just imagine how every-one was laughing at me for trying to defy Paige—or worse, was annoyed at me for refusing to give up more practice time to her. After all, no one expected anything of me, but they expected everything of her.

I glanced around the arena, wondering who else knew about me and Paige. It seemed as if everyone was staring at me, and I could feel myself breathing faster and faster.

Then I felt the coach's reassuring hand on my shoulder. "Easy, Mia," she said. "You're starting to hyperventilate. And you're not even in skates yet."

I reminded myself that, compared to what my

mom faces every day, my own problems were small ones. So I'd have to do what she does: Take things one step at a time. Don't think about Paige. Don't think about the fans. For now, just concentrate on helping Anya and Vanessa—then on getting out on the ice at the right time myself.

"Anya the Skater, I'm Anya the Skater," Anya was murmuring to herself over and over. Trying to work off her nerves, she was fluttering her hands and arms like the blades of a blender.

Seeing Anya in trouble made me forget about myself. "You'll be okay," I said to her and repeated my advice to myself. "Don't think about the arena or the judges or the other skaters. Just focus on one part of the routine at a time. And when that's done, think about the next. Trust our coach and her training, and you'll do fine."

Anya nodded absently as if she'd only half-heard me, but Vanessa had heard. She grumbled to me, "Will you be quiet? I'm trying to visualize my routine."

I'd heard that some skaters try to picture each moment of their performance in their imagination.

"Okay," I said.

"Are you done, Mia?" Coach Schubert asked. When I nodded contritely, she added, speaking to Anya and Vanessa, "Mia happens to be right, though. Don't try to worry about your whole program at the same time. Just do it one step at a time."

"Right," Anya said, looking at Vanessa.

The coach smiled at them. "I just want to let you know that I'm proud of how hard you girls have worked. You've got everything you need to win. So go out and do it."

Anya and Vanessa sailed out with the other skaters in their group to warm up and practice bits of their routines. Vanessa seemed fine on the ice, and Anya was trying to keep it simple by substituting single jumps in place of the double jumps she would do later.

As the group finished, I saw Mr. Knowles hurrying down the steps, hand in hand with Vanessa's mother. When Vanessa and Anya came off the ice, I pointed out her parents to Vanessa. "Amazing," she said, but I realized that she has a pretty smile when she's happy.

Vanessa was the second skater in the group. As Coach Schubert gave her some last-minute instructions, Vanessa never stopped gazing at the ice as she kept picturing herself out there.

Vanessa began well, but then, she always does. She is a strong, fast skater and a great jumper but a lousy lander, so when she whirled up from the ice like a spinning top, I crossed all my fingers and even tried to curl my toes across one another. She twirled through the air but at slightly the wrong angle, so I held my breath when she came down. Luckily, she managed to stay upright as she spun away.

Coach Schubert had created a routine for her that brought out her speed and energy, and I never saw her skate it better. I got exhausted just watching her.

When she came off the ice, I made sure that she turned toward her parents so that she could see them standing up and clapping like crazy.

This time she kept her eyes on them, but she said to me, "Thanks."

"For what?" I asked.

"You're noisy and a real pest sometimes," she sniffed. "But I figured if you were right about my parents, maybe you were right about some other things. After all, what did I have to lose? So I just took things one step at a time, and it worked."

I thought she would go and change and then join her parents, but instead she said she wanted to wait for Anya to finish.

"Good luck," she wished Anya.

"Remember—you're Anya the Skater right now,"

The Skaters

I reminded her, "not Anya Sorokowski."

"Skater, skater, skater," she repeated quickly and softly even when the coach came to give her some last-minute tips. She still looked pretty nervous when she went out onto the ice.

In the stands, Mom put an arm around Mrs. Sorokowski, who looked anxious enough to bite through the chair in front of her. It was just like my brothers had said: a competition can be as hard on the competitors' families as it is on the competitors themselves.

As Anya's music began, her first steps seemed a little stiff, but she softened as soon as she arched backward in a layback spin. One leg raised, she spun in one spot as if she were trying to drill herself into the rink itself.

It is something Anya does well, and she knows it. When she came out of the spin, she seemed to relax—and it showed. If Vanessa's routine had been about power, Anya's was all about grace and balance, and Coach Schubert had planned a program that showcased her skills. And as Vanessa had, Anya performed her program better than I'd ever seen before. Watching Anya sail across the ice was like watching a piece of lovely silk drift in the wind.

When Anya was done, she came off the ice grinning. "It was just the way you said. I didn't feel like my regular self. I was someone who could do anything."

Vanessa hugged Anya—amazing Anya as much as it did me. "That was fantastic, Anya!"

I heard the click of a camera and saw that it was Yvette Polk, leaning over a railing in the nearby stands. She held up a little digital voice recorder in her other hand. "Yoo-hoo, Anya, remember me? Can I interview you and . . . and . . . ?"

"Vanessa Knowles," Vanessa said.

"I want to get some of your thoughts for my fanzine," Yvette explained.

Suddenly shy again, Anya asked Vanessa, "Do you want to?"

"Sure. Let's enjoy our moment while we can. So wave," Vanessa urged.

When Anya was a little slow to obey, Vanessa raised Anya's hand for her, and Yvette immediately snapped another picture.

12

The Buzz

Anya and Vanessa were lucky to have skated so early. Their work was now done and they could sit back and enjoy themselves, because everyone was figuring that at the end, it was going to be Paige and her group on the podium anyway.

Even so, people both in the seats and in the waiting area were talking about Anya and Vanessa. I overheard Paige's friend, the blonde girl, ask, "I didn't expect those Lucerne skaters to place so high after I saw their practices, did you?"

"Some skaters save their best stuff for the competitions," one of the girls said.

Paige was chewing a nail. "I just hope I'm one of them. There's nothing like it when you win at figure skating, and there's really nothing like it when you lose."

Yesterday at practice, Paige had seemed confident enough, but now I wondered how much of it was just an act, like Vanessa's. But I told myself that that was impossible. Super Skater had nothing to be scared of.

What I had to hope was that I hadn't left my

"best stuff" at the practice myself. "Do you want me to help you stretch?" Coach Schubert asked.

I shook my head. "Isn't it great about Vanessa and Anya? It's a real feather in your cap."

But with her typical unselfishness, the coach was thinking about her skaters and not herself. "Please don't worry about me," she insisted. "Think about what *you* have to do."

This was my job right now. It was what I'd been working on for these past two years. I felt myself brimming over with nervous energy, so I straightened like a soldier at attention and snapped off a salute. "Yes, ma'am."

"Save the attitude for the rink," the coach laughed as she handed me my MP3 player.

I put its buds into my ears, listening to the music and feeling how my arms and legs were almost twitching to respond.

Finally, it was time for my group to warm up. After the long wait, I was glad to get out on the ice. As I glided outward with the five other girls, I breathed in the cold, chill air as gratefully as a fish would take in the water of a lake. This was my real home. This was where I belonged, where I could leave all my worries behind me.

The Buzz

We'd had only that one chance to actually perform in the arena, so it was nice to be able to do the
brief versions of our programs. At least that's what
you're supposed to do, but it's hard to concentrate
fully on your program because of all the other skaters.
There's no official etiquette for avoiding collisions on
the ice, but the coach had told me that if I saw someone
going up into a jump, I should steer clear.

So when I saw a blonde girl begin a double toe
just ahead of me, I broke off my own routine and curled
around her. It was only when I thought I was in an open
space that I started to get ready to do my double lutz.
But suddenly, from the corner of my eye, I glimpsed a
blurry something barreling toward me fast. I'd played
so many games of hockey with my brothers that I didn't
stop to think but reacted instinctively, twisting away so
that Paige narrowly missed me.

At first, I thought she had just made a mistake,
but from the way she grinned at me over her shoulder,
I realized she had done it deliberately.

I wound up doing just a single, but then I got
ahold of myself. I couldn't let something like that
throw me off. I've learned from competing against my
brothers that you lose if you let their antics get to you.
Instead of getting angry, you keep on with your plan,

using that emotion as an extra boost.

When the warm-up time was over, Coach
Schubert was waiting for me as I exited. Mom had
come over to the railing in the stands next to the
waiting area. As the coach handed me the guards for
my skates and my warm-up sweater, Mom fumed,
"That Paige girl practically threw a body check at
Mia. Can't we file a complaint?"

"Why? She just told everyone, including the
judges, that she's scared of Mia," the coach announced.

I blinked my eyes. "No disrespect, Coach, but it's
definitely the other way around."

"You don't waste time intimidating your
opponents unless you think there's a real chance
they can beat you," the coach explained.

I wasn't sure who was crazier, the coach or Paige,
but I made sure to smile and nod at Paige when I saw
her, again pretending to be more confident than I felt.

Then all I could do was kill time, pacing to work
off some of my nervous energy.

"Here," the coach said, handing me a note. "Your
mom told me to wait until now to give this to you.
Maybe this will take your mind off the competition for
a while."

The envelope and paper had the embossed acorn

of the hotel stationery. Mom had written:

I just want you to know that you have been a
source of joy and pride over the years as you've grown
from a stumbling infant into such a fine young lady.
Every day, I marvel at how fortunate I am. XOX

I wished Mom could have been there with me so I could tell her that I am the lucky one, but instead all I could do was smile and wave the note at her where she had rejoined the Sorokowskis in the stands.

The coach held out my music player to me again, but I shook my head. I was curious about how the other skaters in my group were going to do, and yet I didn't want to watch them.

I probably checked and rechecked my bootlaces a dozen times before the blonde girl came back with her coach. "How could you lose your nerve like that?" he asked, shaking his head in exasperation.

"I just knew I didn't have the double jump," she defended herself. "It was safer to do a single." But she was almost in tears.

And the black-haired girl actually was crying after she was done because she'd fallen twice. Even if she had snubbed Vanessa, I felt sorry for her. After all, that could be me in just a short while.

I glanced at Paige, but she was biting her nails again. For all the notice she gave her friends at that moment, she might have been the only person on earth. I don't think she even heard the advice that Coach McManus was giving her.

So maybe Coach Schubert was right. Paige really could feel nervous and scared just like me. That meant she was human after all. And if she was human, I had a slim chance against her.

Another girl went out, but from the disappointed expression on her face when she came back, she must not have skated all that well.

And then Paige was handing her bottle of water to her coach and heading toward the ice.

As I sat on a chair, gripping the seat, I tried to think only about my routine, but I could hear Paige's music start. And then the applause grew louder and louder until the crowd was roaring. I'd seen Paige's routine during practice, so I already knew the different elements she was performing. But today she must have been sensational to wow the crowd like that.

Even before she came back beaming, I knew she must have skated a dazzling program, maybe good enough for first.

And that scared me. How was I supposed to compete with her?

I looked down at my hands. My knuckles had turned white from clutching the seat. And I was so frightened that I didn't want to let go.

13

The Routine

Coach Schubert touched my elbow. "It's time."
She was already on her feet.

I was so used to doing what Coach Schubert said
that even though I had intended to stay put, my hands
released their grip on the seat and my body got up and
followed her before my brain could stop it.

As we neared the door, the arena was buzzing
like a giant beehive about Paige's performance. Now
that they had seen the Superstar, the spectators were
stretching or getting snacks, impatient for the remaining
skaters to finish so that the scores could be posted and
the official medal ceremony could begin.

I felt like obliging the audience by skipping my
turn and hiding backstage instead—say, for the rest of
my life. I had been so distracted by Paige's tantrum the
other day that I hadn't really noticed how vast the ice
in the arena was. It spread before me now like a shining
white sea, making me feel like a tiny, insignificant bug. I
had no right to be here with skaters like Paige. The odds
were stacked against me.

Then I thought of how hard Mom and Dad work

every day to beat the long odds stacked against our whole family. And then I remembered a hockey game where Perry had battled his way with the puck through the opposing team. With the tournament on the line and the score tied with thirty seconds to go, he had made the goal. And what about that time when Skip was a goalie and he had three opponents bearing down on him with the puck during a power play? He couldn't have been any less scared than I was now—and yet he'd shut them out.

So what if I *was* the underdog here? I should be used to it after years of playing against my brothers. If it meant I had to skate better than I ever had before in my life, then that's what I'd try to do.

Suddenly my fear changed to extra adrenaline. I couldn't wait to get out there on the ice and show everyone that the St. Clairs don't know the meaning of the word *quit*. I headed for the ice.

"Whoa," the coach said, grabbing my arm. "Take off your guards first."

Ears burning, I snatched them off my blades.

Chuckling, the coach took the guards from me. "Don't be embarrassed. A coach waits her entire life for a student who loves to compete the way you do. Your parents raised a skater with a big heart—you've got a bigger heart than anyone I've ever met."

As I skated out onto the ice, I borrowed another tip from the coach and hummed Zuzu's jingle, "We're Just Nuts About Sewing," to help calm my nerves. Suddenly I heard my brothers giving loud whoops. With them was Dad with his hands high overhead as he began to clap. They had managed to make it after all. *Of course.* And on either side were Bob and Mona, a bright burst of pink that was Nelda, Anya and her family . . . and I even saw Vanessa and her parents.

"Sic 'em, Tiger!" Mom shouted.

With them cheering me on, there was no way I could turn tail and run. It was just as Coach Schubert had said: the right audience can make a skater rise above what she would normally do.

As I slid toward the center, I glanced down at the new boots that Bob and the Lucerne staff had given me. And I touched the flowing, floaty dress that Coach Schubert and Mom had made, and that Nelda had made possible.

As I stopped and struck my pose, I realized that my brothers were wrong: I wasn't out there by myself. I was part of a team. I'd always been part of a team. My parents, family, and friends had been helping me all these years. My coach had passed on what she had learned so painfully during her career. And the staff at the Lucerne thought of me as one of their own. I wasn't just skating for myself but for all of them. They just couldn't be on the ice with me. So I'd try to do my best—not only for myself but for them as well.

As I curled my wrists, my heart began thumping crazily. Closing my eyes, I tapped out a few bars of "Lady of Spain" on the keys of an invisible accordion. It's the song that helps me settle down and focus before skating. In my imagination, I was small again, sitting on Dad's lap with the accordion, feeling totally safe. I knew that in the next couple of minutes, I couldn't do anything wrong in my parents' eyes. Or my brothers'. Or my friends'.

In fact, I really could have come out there with the guards on my skates and plopped on the rink and they wouldn't have laughed. Instead, they would have rushed out to pick me up. With that kind of support, how could I feel alone?

The first notes of *Swan Lake* drifted down from the speakers, and my body moved forward all on its own, as it had been trained to do during all those long hours of practice. The hissing of my blades mixed with the notes in its own snakelike rhythm.

Sure, I was nervous, but the excitement made

me feel more alert rather than afraid. On the wall of the rink, I saw Zuzu beaming at me from a large advertisement for Nelda's Notions. I took that as a sign of good luck for sure.

Then, taking my cue from the music, I brought my right leg up at the proper time. Swinging it around, I rose into the air for a flying camel spin. Spreading my arms and legs outward, I whirled above the ice like a kite caught in a hurricane. If I had stopped to think, I would have realized that the human body wasn't meant to be flung about like a kite, but my foot was already reaching down automatically toward the ice.

I felt the jar as the blade bit into the surface, and for a fraction of a second I teetered, but then I managed to find the blade's sweet spot that the coach had shown me. As I felt myself starting to turn, I knew I would be all right.

When my leg began to twist, I felt my new boot grip my ankle, tight and solid. Leaning forward, I brought my other leg up as I spun along the ice. Beneath me, I saw the tracks of another skater, one place pitted where someone's blades had stabbed in deep before a jump.

It didn't matter. Those skaters were gone. This was *my* ice now, and I felt as if I could do anything on it.

The Routine

It must have been a pretty flying camel spin, because I heard people applauding around the rink, strangers who didn't know me. It was like being Zuzu all over again, but this time I wasn't dressed up as a squirrel. This time the clapping was for *me* and what I was doing. No, not just for me—any more than when Rick made a goal, he did it by himself. It took a whole team to get him in place to make the goal, and it took a whole team to get me here on the ice, to this moment.

Some flakes of ice had landed on my cheek during the spin, and the cold made me feel extra alive as I headed into my double lutz. The spectators' faces started to blur as I picked up speed and lifted one leg before I kicked off from the ice, rising higher and higher above the rink like a rocket. Snatching my arms in, I pressed them tight against me and crossed my legs as I started to spin like a human top. Once. Twice.

And then I was spreading my arms again, one leg automatically slipping down into position, and looking ahead as I landed, knee bending under the impact and then, as I straightened, using the force to send me speeding onward.

I wasn't worried about making mistakes any-more, only about how I could perform the next step better than the last one. Just as I had felt at the winter show, it was like trying to herd butterflies. It was so difficult it was crazy, but this was what I wanted to do. This was what my family and I had worked for.

So when it was time for my double loop, I leapt into the air like a dolphin for the sheer joy of being alive.

I floated through the rest of my program, feeling as light as the lovely notes hovering in the air. If *Swan Lake* could have played in an endless loop, I would have skated on forever. But I knew my music and my moment were drawing to an end, and that made me feel happy and sad simultaneously. I spun one last time, head up, back straight and proud, arms reaching toward the sky.

All too soon the last beautiful note faded away, its echo ringing around the rink.

And then I was done.

As I stood there panting, I heard the applause begin, rolling toward me from all sides like the waves of an ocean.

14

The Start

They didn't post the scores until thirty minutes after the last skater finished, and there was already a big crowd around the bulletin board by the time Anya, Vanessa, and I got there. It took a bit of wriggling to get to the list with the standings.

Anya was second! I couldn't have felt happier if I'd placed there myself.

Vanessa was fifth. And then I blinked, not believing my own score. I'd come in fourth!

I wasn't surprised to see that Paige was in first place, but a mere tenth of a point separated each of the top six skaters from one another. A cleaner landing on a jump, a straighter back in a skating move, and two of us would have swapped places.

I'd seen so many other great skaters that day that I hadn't really counted on finishing that high. I mean, I'd *hoped* a little, but I hadn't expected it.

Anya and I yelled so loudly that we probably cracked a few ceiling tiles, and then Coach Schubert shepherded us and Vanessa over to Coach McManus and Paige to congratulate them. There was a small mob of well-wishers around them, but they parted when they saw us, and some of them even complimented us as we passed.

Coach McManus noticed us first and tapped his student's shoulder so that she turned to face us. "Congratulations," I said, holding out my hand.

"And to you," Paige said, taking mine. "And you, too," she said to Anya as she shook hers. "We're going to be bumping heads a lot from now on." She looked past us at Vanessa. "And good job, Vivien."

"Actually, it's Vanessa," she corrected Paige, but by then Yvette Polk had already claimed Paige's attention.

As we walked away, Vanessa gave us a twisted grin. "Well, at least she sort of notices me now."

"She'll remember your name when you beat her," I promised.

Vanessa laughed at that. "Well, if I had to lose to anyone, I'm glad it's you two. But just wait until next time."

"You were all splendid, girls," Coach Schubert said. She looked tired but happy, and she was already sounding a little hoarse. Since this was just the start for her at Regionals, I hoped her voice would hold up, because she had a lot more skaters to coach after us.

She continued, "Now that you know you can hold your own against the competition, I'm going to push you even harder to improve."

"Is that a compliment or a threat?" I asked.

"Both." The coach grinned.

Vanessa's parents were waiting as we climbed up into the stands. Mr. Knowles pumped Coach Schubert's hand enthusiastically. "It's a great beginning for the Lucerne at Regionals," he chirped. "Yes, sir, a great beginning. And I'm a big enough man to admit that I was wrong about you. You're definitely the right person for the job."

"Thank you," the coach said cautiously. "That means a lot."

He whipped out a small notebook. "Now, I jotted down some ideas for Vanessa's next routine."

"Dad-dee," Vanessa said, grabbing his arm, "that can wait. Let me enjoy today at least."

"You've got to strike while the iron's hot, kitten," her father objected. But with a nod, Mrs. Knowles seized his other arm, and she and Vanessa dragged him toward the exit—with him protesting all the way.

By then, some other coaches and parents had come over to Coach Schubert, and with a wave, Anya and I left her to this other part of her job and went on to find our families and friends. After we had hugged everyone, I got down to the business of grilling Dad and my brothers. "Where were you guys? What took you so long to get here?"

Dad pointed over his head toward a skybox. "Oh, we were here. Just up yonder."

"You should have been there, Sis," Rick bubbled. "Chairs so plush, they swallowed you up like quicksand."

"And the fridge was stocked with every kind of soda," Skip added.

"And snacks," Perry said, smacking his lips. I was sure he'd made a serious dent in them.

"I called in a few favors from my buddies here," Bob said.

"Well, it was great being up there," Dad said to him, "so thanks."

"But," Rick added, "when we realized you couldn't hear us cheering, we made the ultimate sacrifice. We left all that comfort and came down here to mix with the peasants."

"It really made a big difference to me," I said, "so thanks for doing that."

"We thought it would," Nelda said. She circled me, inspecting the dress critically. "I think I'm going to

"Three cheers for Mia!" Rick called out. "Bravo!"

call this the Mia Special. You did Zuzu proud."

"You did *us* proud, Sis," Skip said, grabbing my shoulders. The next moment, Dad and my brothers had hoisted me into the air.

"Three cheers for Mia!" Rick called out. "Bravo!"

Heads started to turn as my friends and family cheered, raising me high above them with each cheer. When that was finished and I'd been set back on my feet, I glimpsed shy Anya trying to sneak away.

"And three cheers for Anya!" I said, grabbing her arm.

She turned red as a beet. "Please don't make me," Anya begged.

"Sorry," I said, "but this is the price of success in my family." I dragged her toward her fans and her fate. "People may not remember our skating, but they'll certainly remember our celebrations."

"Folks're going to remember a lot of things about you, girls," Dad predicted. "This is only the start of a big future for the both of you."

If Dad's prophecy comes true, I will owe it all to my family and my friends.

And then I was helping my brothers lift Anya into the air as I joined everyone in cheering for her at the top of my lungs.

Real Girls,
Real Letters

American Girl receives hundreds of letters a week from girls asking for help. Here are some real letters from real girls who are learning to develop their talents—and to compete in healthy ways.

To: American Girl
From: Bad Sport
Subject: Good Sportsmanship

Dear American Girl,
I was in a track program with my friend
last year. I beat her in every race. This
year, she is beating *me* in every race.
I know I should congratulate her, but
I just can't! Instead I get mad.

Instead of measuring yourself against others, use your
competitive energy to set personal goals, such as beating
your *own* best time, and try to reach those. Being a good
athlete isn't just about winning; it's also about being
a good sport and a supportive teammate.
If you're disappointed in your time, take
a minute and cool off in private. Then
challenge yourself to congratulate
your friend the way you'd like to be
congratulated. Remember—if you're
giving it your all and accepting your
times with confidence and grace, then
you're a winner—no matter what the
stopwatch says.

Following Your Heart

Dear American Girl,
I'm in a sport that most girls aren't in, and I'm afraid that people won't like me for this.
—Karate Girl

If someone doesn't like you because you do karate, then he or she is not a good friend. If karate is right for you—you enjoy it, you're growing stronger and healthier because of it, and you're working with others who also enjoy it—then just go for it. Although it can be hard to follow a path that's a bit different, you are not alone—there *are* other girls and women who excel at karate! When you meet other girls in your classes or at competitions, make a point of getting to know them. But enjoy your friendships with the boys you train with, too. Common interests can create strong friendships!

Behind the Scenes

Dear American Girl,
My two best friends and I tried out for a play.
They both got parts and I didn't. I feel so left
out when they talk about rehearsals at school.
I don't know what to say.
          —Bad Actress

Feeling "out of the loop" is hard, but being onstage isn't the only way to be part of a play. Talk to the director about helping with lighting, scenery, costumes, or makeup. Be as supportive as possible to your friends, but don't be afraid to sometimes say, "Hey, can we change the subject?" if the play is becoming the only topic of conversation. And take heart; the play will be over soon enough. Your friendships, however, could last a lifetime.

Competition

Dear American Girl,
There is a new boy in my class and he's really good at drawing. I used to be the artist of the class, but nobody likes my drawings anymore.
—Jealous

Just because this boy is good at art doesn't mean that you aren't, too. Competition can be rough, but it can also inspire you to improve, so don't get discouraged. Keep working on your art and developing your own style. Focus less on your classmates' comments and more on feeling good about your own growth as an artist.

Oh, Brothers!

Dear American Girl,
I have a huge problem. I'm the only girl in a family of boys! I have no one to play with. I'm tired of watching TV. What should I do?
—No one 2 play with

Just because they're boys doesn't mean you can't play with your brothers. You know that girls can do anything that boys can, so instead of sitting on the sidelines, join in! Or better yet, invite them to join you in an outdoor game. Stop thinking of activities as "for boys" or "for girls," and you'll have more fun. And so will your brothers!

To: American Girl
From: Worst Player
Subject: Stay or go?

Dear American Girl,
I am in basketball, but I'm no good.
Should I quit, or stay?

There are many roles on a team, and being the most skilled
player is only one of them. Before you quit, ask yourself a
few questions: What drew you to basketball in the first place?
Are your skills getting better, even if you're not the best
player? What else do you bring to the team—are you
the heart or spirit of the team, and do you
offer your teammates much-needed
support? Is your body stronger
and healthier because you
play? Are you learning to
work as part of a group?
And most important of
all—is it fun? If you
answered yes to some
of these questions,
stay on the team.

Meet the Author

Laurence Yep has published more than sixty
books, and recently he won the
Laura Ingalls Wilder medal for his
contribution to children's literature.
He has been a fan of figure skating
since childhood, when he went to
see mummies in a museum
connected to a skating rink. He
wound up watching the figure skaters instead.
He is very proud of his official Kristi Yamaguchi
bobblehead doll.